Steampunk

Fairy

Tales

Angela Castillo, Chris Champe,

Leslie & David T. Allen, Allison Latzko,

Heather White, Ashley Capes, Daniel Lind

Cover design: Indigo Forest Deigns
http://indigoforest.weebly.com/

Copy editor: Heather White

ISBN: 153060902X
ISBN-13: 978-1530609024

.

Contents

Preface

Imagine how your favorite fairy tales would be told by an advanced Victorian society that's powered by steam.

That was the idea Angela Castillo proposed in our online writing community. She handpicked six other writers to contribute and provided few restrictions. It wasn't until weeks later we realized that, even with such a small group, the authors represented three continents and were retelling myths from Germany, England, France, Italy, and Japan.

Some stories stay close to their roots, while others have familiar elements but come with a twist. When reading, make a little game of it: see if you can guess the fairy tale. Some are classics, others are obscure, and a few might not be circulated in your culture. You can check your guesses at the end of the book.

One thread unites them all: each tale is a reimagining of how it would be told from a steam-driven society. Please, enjoy.

If you would like to learn more about steampunk, please see wikipedia.org/wiki/Steampunk

The Clockwork People

Angela Castillo

Old Man Streusel knew about the magic in his toy shop. It whispered in his ear and sent dancing breezes to tickle his nose even when the doors and windows were closed.

When customers entered the building, the magic settled on their cheeks in a warm glow. Most adults wrote it off as happy childhood memories brought on by the colorful toys, but the children knew better. They stared at Streusel with wide eyes and he would wink.

Whirs and clicks filled the shop, for Streusel had bestowed the gift of movement to every toy. Tin cows kicked over the tin pails of anguished tin milkmaids. Miniature trains belched steam as they rushed across tiny tracks. Engines in horseless carriages, sized for mouse drivers, chugged and clunked when curious children cranked the front handles.

Streusel's joy was only complete when the shop was full of happy children. He would wrap up one toy after another, whispering a blessing with each as he sent them off to new homes.

The toy shop was located in a large village built around a great factory, with giant rows of smokestacks that belched black clouds into the heavens. This company was owned by a kind man who cared for people and made sure each employee was paid fairly and not overworked.

On paydays, tired factory workers stepped into the cozy shop on the way home to choose toys for their children.

Most days, Streusel created many toys at once, like a one-man factory. He'd set out gears, frames and various metal shapes to form rows of boats, trains or dolls.

But Pieter was different.

Pieter was a clockwork doll. His body was formed from hammered tin and his inner workings created from the gears and cogs of a discarded cuckoo clock. Streusel had made dolls that could wave, twist and bow, but Pieter could do all three and then some. Streusel spent months on the toy, bending pieces this way and that, often staying up far into the night to frown over a tiny scrap of metal. Since Streusel had no family of his own, he poured all the love his lonely heart possessed into the little doll.

Finished at last, he sat the tiny man in a place of honor beside the cash register.

Pieter charmed all the customers with his bright red cap and green coat. Whenever a child came into the shop, Streusel would turn the tiny key in his back and Pieter would go through a special routine. He would remove his hat, bow and dance a jig—fast at first, then slower and slower as the clockwork ran down.

Children clapped and squealed in delight, and parents would ask, "How much?"

Streusel always folded his arms, shook his head, and beamed until his round cheeks turned pink. "Not for sale," he would say. "He's my special one."

He had almost completed Gerta, his clockwork woman, when he noticed a change in Pieter.

Sometimes when he'd turn the key, Pieter's antics went on after the clockwork wound down. On occasion the toy would give an extra bow or wave. When Streusel was alone in the shop, working on Gerta's parts, he'd hear a quiet '*creak*.' He'd look up to see Pieter's tiny face turned toward him, his shiny, painted eyes gazing at him with an extra twinkle Streusel hadn't added with a brush.

Adjusting the setting on his workman's goggles, the old man always checked the toy over to see if he'd overlooked a flaw causing these strange movements. The magic tickled the back of his mind, reminding him of its presence.

Gerta progressed much faster then Pieter, being Streusel's second doll of the kind. By the time he'd put the finishing touches on her blue milkmaid dress and formed the pink flower for her golden metal curls, Streusel could no longer deny the truth.

11

The magic of the toyshop had settled into Pieter's tin heart. Streusel wasn't frightened when Pieter clanked over the tabletop to him and made a bow so deep his cap almost brushed the wooden surface. After all, the toyshop was a place of joy and happiness, and therefore could only create good magic.

From then on, when Streusel polished and painted and tweaked, he would hear little snaps and creaks and look up to see Pieter standing beside him, watching in apparent fascination.

Then came the night he placed the completed Gerta beside Pieter. Pieter placed a hand on Gerta's tin shoulder and made a creaking sound.

Streusel's eyes widened. Though quiet, the doll had clearly said, "Hello."

A shudder ran through Gerta's tin form. Her head turned. "Hello!" she creaked back.

Pieter took Gerta's hand, and together they bowed before Streusel. "Father," they said in unison.

The following days were filled with fun. While Streusel tinkered at his work bench, the little dolls played hide-and-seek among the tools and parts, calling to each other in tiny voices. At night, they snuggled in doll beds while Streusel read them bedtime stories. When customers came into the shop, they would 'play dollies' as they called it, entertaining the children with their funny routines. Parents begged Streusel for a price, and he would always refuse. How could he sell his children?

One day, a dark cloud settled over the town. The factory owner who had cared so much for his workers died. A wealthy man from a land far away purchased the factory from the family of the deceased.

Whispered stories began to drift through the streets about injuries from faulty machinery. Wages began to spiral down, and those who complained were fired and sent out into the street.

Workers trudged by Streusel's toy shop on weary feet with no extra coins in their pockets for such trivial things as toys. The children would press cold noses to the shop windows to gaze at the forbidden treasures.

Only a few weeks after this turn of events, Streusel sat at his counter, sliding the few pennies he'd managed to collect into a tin box. Pieter and Gerta stood before him, dancing their prettiest jig. He forced himself to smile. *What do they know of this cruel world?* The magic in the shop had weakened from the sadness, but the dolls remained happy and full of joy.

Not long after, Streusel was forced to give up his peaceful life. He sold his remaining toys for pennies. An old woman bought the shop to turn into a day-old bread store. With this money, Streusel knew he could survive for a short time.

One of Streusel's good friends owned the theater in the middle of town. He offered Streusel the small loft above for help with building repairs. When the toymaker arrived, he unpacked his few possessions and placed them around the tiny apartment. Last, he pulled out his greatest treasure: the cardboard box containing the two clockwork dolls and their beds.

The toys stretched and looked around them in bewilderment.

"Father, where is the workshop? Where are the children?" Pieter asked.

Streusel began to cry in great, heaving sobs, and the toys patted him and laid their cold, tin heads against his tear-stained cheeks.

Every day, Streusel went out to look for work. He was too old for the factories to consider and all the shop owners would shake their heads in regret. Sometimes he sold small parcels of firewood he had gathered from the woods near town. More often he brought Pieter and Greta out to the streets. They could attract a reasonable crowd and bring smiles to the most dismal of faces with their antics.

After dancing merry jigs or doing acrobatics, the dolls pretended to wind down with hats outstretched. Children pleaded with parents, and someone in the crowd always produced a spare penny so Streusel could wind them up again.

When he walked home each day, Streusel struggled with the guilt of bringing his children back to the gloomy apartment, but when he saw the pinched faces of neighborhood children he would comfort himself by thinking, *at least my children will never go hungry.*

One gloomy day, rain drenched the dreary streets and left a maze of puddles in its wake. Streusel almost chose to stay home, but his stomach rumbled and it was too wet to gather wood dry enough to sell. So he picked up the cardboard box and stepped down the narrow, dark staircase to the ground floor of the theater. Tinny voices strained through the walls of the box while the dolls talked in excitement about the children they would see that day. Streusel held the box closer to his ear.

"I love you, Pieter."

"And I love you, Gerta."

Streusel chuckled to himself. It never ceased to fill him with wonder, these tiny people who had come into his life. *Ah. They are dolls. What could they possibly understand about love?*

He found an awning by a busy street to set up for the day. Despite the mist, quite a few people scurried through the lanes, and soon the clockwork dolls performed for a larger crowd than ever. They emptied their tiny caps into Streusel's big one, and before long it was jingling with coins.

The happy event was interrupted by a child's cry. "Run for your lives!"

A black carriage crashed through the crowd, drawn by four ebony steeds. The coachman had neglected their bits and foam mixed with blood streamed from the cobalt mouths while they reared and plunged through the mud in a wild-eyed frenzy.

People screamed and scattered. Streusel's dolls stood in the middle of the street where they had been kicked by the frightened children's feet.

Streusel pleaded from the side, "Come to me! Come, my children!" but they could not hear him through the madness. Hand in hand, they ran in the wrong direction, under the wicked wheels of the carriage.

The coach clattered away, and the street cleared. No one saw Old Man Streusel when he bent to collect the broken parts of his dolls.

He trudged home and cleaned the mud from the twisted pieces of tin as best he could. Placing them back in the cardboard box, he decided to bury them in a quiet place after the rain stopped. The air in the room rested on his shoulders like a leaden shawl. Every spark of magic had been sucked away.

"Now, I have lost everything," he wept.

The next morning, dawn poked a cold finger through the apartment's single, small window. A scratching sound came from the box.

"Not a rat!" he howled. "This is the absolute worst!" He picked up the box with the intent to fling the filthy animal against the wall.

A breezy bit of magic swirled past his face and blew open the top of the lid.

Pieter's shiny brown eyes stared up from the box.

The old man stared in wonder at a perfectly formed clockwork child with golden curls, Gerta's dimpled cheeks, and a jumper of green and blue.

The child waved a tin hand. "Hello!"

Perfection

Chris Champe

The gala was in full swing, with the players on stage the center of the entire production. Not only for their music, but the act of playing itself was something to behold. They moved in perfect harmony, each and every motion, no matter how small, matched flawlessly across the entire stage. Fingers brushed across strings with a smooth surety that could never be found in nature. The pianist's hands flew over the keys with absolute efficiency.

Of course, there were murmurings among the crowd.

Those who felt the motions were unnatural. Those who felt it lacked the human element.

Of course it did.

It was simple fact that humans were flawed. Why else would they build machines to act in their place if not because machines were better suited to the task? Why reject the unnatural, as though nature were the final authority on how things ought to be done? Wasn't the rejection of and improvement upon nature the entire course of human progress?

If one were so eager to embrace nature over ingenuity, perhaps one should abandon medicine, clothing, and shelter; avoid all those conveniences of the modern world, and take up life in a cave somewhere deep in a forest. Arguments about the superiority of nature would not stand so strong against a winter in the elements, or sleep disturbed by the all-too-near howling of wolves.

Mary blinked and steered her thoughts away from the morbid turn they had taken, and turned her focus back to the performance. It was hardly unusual for her to become lost in thought since her accident, but her mind rarely took such dark paths. Instead, her daydreams were typically focused upon more immediate concerns, such as how she might occupy herself for the day, or what great work her dear husband was currently perfecting.

Perfection in all things was her husband's eternal drive, and these were merely his most recent attempt at achieving it. The entire band was composed of automata, something that had long been considered impossible, for no machine could properly imitate the smooth, controlled motions of human talent. Their mobility had always been a rough, jerky, haphazard affair. It was a brave man who allowed an automaton to serve the tea, or, at least, one very forgiving of stains. Giving it an instrument was merely an exercise in recreating the confused cacophony that a small child would produce, given the same opportunity.

This new design, though …. It was not enough that they move as humans could. That would have never satisfied her husband, and he had confessed to her that he had mastered *that* challenge months before. But no, he strove further. His work was not complete until his creations combined the precision of the machine with the grace of the flesh, into a final product greater than either of its parts.

And not only were their motions stunning, but their appearance as well: the polished metal of the limbs, highlighted by the faint glow of the luminiferous relays beneath, carrying energy from the zevatron core to the brilliantly complex mechanisms which drove their motion. The new cores, designed to last a lifetime in typical applications, were one of the few aspects of the automata that were not her husband's design. Aetheric energy was one of the handful of fields he conducted no work in, and that her husband considered this new model from his friend Mr. Lorentz satisfactory for his work spoke volumes of its capability. Even with her limited understanding of the technology, Mary was aware that Lorentz's design improved upon the older Mosley model by an order of magnitude.

But it was not the glistening of metal or the shine of aetheric energy that drew her eyes most of all. What she had been focused upon for near the entirety of her little daydream had been the hands of the pianist automaton. She had been a keen student of the instrument herself, once, though she had not been able to play since her accident. She watched those brass and steel fingers dance across the keys for a few minutes longer, then closed her eyes and placed her hands upon an imaginary keyboard, picturing, in her mind, the feel of the ivory as she found her place and began to play.

Or as she attempted to play.

However she pictured the keys in her mind, however well she recalled old scores, however certain she was of where her fingers ought to next land, her limbs simply refused to cooperate. The motions she made felt… *awkward*. Restrained, somehow, as though she did not have quite the control of her body that she was accustomed to. She let a scowl mar her face as she redoubled her efforts at focusing upon her imaginary performance, but the more she tried to force her body's cooperation, the more awkward and exaggerated her motions became, furthering her frustrations ever more.

Suddenly, strong hands grasped her own, holding them in place. Her eyes flew open to meet the steely grey of her husband's. In the corners of her vision, she could see several guests watching her, expressions ranging from interest, to concern, to the blend of scorn and embarrassment usually reserved for the mentally ill when they failed to compose themselves in public.

"Darling, you're drawing stares," her husband said quietly to her. "Are you alright?"

Why? She had merely been …. She shook her head. Her thoughts were growing muddled, a frequent result of overstressing herself. She hadn't been playing, had she? No, she was attending the party. The automaton was the one playing.

"I … I'm fine, dear," she said, pulling back slightly from his hands, though he didn't relax his grip. "I was merely … recalling playing on my own piano."

He nodded. "I thought as much. I've told you before, you have yet to fully recover from your accident, and you're in no shape to be playing now."

Mary's eyes drifted back towards the artificial player on the stage, who, along with its bandmates, kept up the music, unconcerned with the scene playing out before them. "I was so good, then …. How could I lose all of it?"

"You were perfect." He took one of her hands to his lips and kissed it, then released her other hand to put his upon her back. "And we'll have you perfect again soon enough. But you mustn't concern yourself with your piano. Attempting it could strain your body, and the stress would strain the mind. For now, it's best that you have a rest. You've worked yourself up."

"I'm fine, though, dear," she objected, though she couldn't muster the will for more than a token resistance when her husband began guiding her towards the door. "I could stay and watch the musicians a bit longer."

He shook his head. "No, that's what set you into this spell to begin with. Come along, you need to lie down and have a rest."

She gave in and allowed her husband to walk her from the floor, the eyes of several partygoers following them as they left, though only one said anything as they passed.

"Is something the matter, Blaubart?" asked a man who she did not recognize, though something made her feel she should have.

"Just a bit of overstimulation, Lorentz, despite an ongoing weakness." Doctor Blaubart gave a resigned chuckle. "You know how they can be."

"One of the many fields where your experience outweighs mine. But take care of her. We'll talk when you're back."

Her husband pulled her away again, out of the ballroom and into a small lounge just down the hall— near enough that she could hear the festivities, but far enough that she wouldn't be part of them.

"Here you are, darling," he said, laying her down on a chaise lounge under the window, from which she could see the moon above.

She didn't resist. In fact, she felt quite exhausted. Hadn't she been so excited for the party just a few minutes ago? Why was she so tired?

"Rest now," her husband said. "You're nearly back to perfect condition, but until that day comes, we must be wary of these little hiccups. You understand?"

She was merely able to nod.

"Good," he said, and smoothed her hair before standing. "I'll come back to tend to you, but for now, I must still play the host. You'll be safe here."

He turned and left the room, closing and locking the door behind him. It was indicative of just how near this room was to the party that she could hear the conversation pick up back in the ballroom.

"The things you burden yourself with, Blaubart, I will never understand."

"We all have our fixations, though, don't we? By the way, the amount of light released by your zevatron core and relays must terribly hamper the efficiency."

"It does, but when the work is so brilliant, some excess should be permitted in making a spectacle of it."

"You're proving my point. Though more importantly, I may find cause to modify the design, and would appreciate your input. I find myself needing much smoother output modulation for restricting energy flow."

She lost the flow of their conversation in its ever-increasing technicality, and soon was unconscious of anything at all.

###

Mary found herself idly wandering the halls of the manor. She did her best not to become upset. That was bad for her condition, as her forced departure from the party … two? No, three days prior had so aptly demonstrated. She paused there, tapping a finger against the frame of a painting as she composed herself. Her husband had been right to remove her. She had been growing over-excited and lightheaded. She might have collapsed or had a fit, had he not done it.

Knowing that, though, did nothing to dull the sting of being taken from the music, and from watching a pianist, however artificial, display the same mastery over that instrument she once had.

It was worsened by being unable to play her own.

She had spent uncountable hours whiling away the time in these halls as she recovered, a process that now seemed interminable, and in that time, she was certain she had read and read again every book, examined in detail every piece of art, and explored every crevice of their home. She had grown bored with it all ages ago, but still managed to find some way or another to distract herself enough from her situation.

However, in the wake of the incident at the party, and her inability to recall how to play the piano, she knew of only one thing that would satisfy her, and that was to play on her own instrument once again.

She had gone to the drawing room where her prized piano had stood for so long opposite the ancient stone fireplace, but found that a simple desk now occupied the space that once belonged to the instrument. She eventually cornered one of the few serving-girls who hadn't irritated her husband and been dismissed in favor of an automaton, yet.

"Girl, what has been done with the piano?" she asked the servant, a pretty young thing who'd been with them for some time, but whose name entirely slipped Mary's mind.

"The piano, madam?" The girl paused and stared at her, a look of confusion, but which also held a bit of what she'd seen in the party guests who witnessed her episode.

"Yes, the piano. *My* piano. It was here not long ago. Has it been moved?"

The girl's confusion visibly deepened, and she shook her head. "Madam, this room has been the same since I started here. There's never been a piano."

Mary took a breath and swallowed her irritation with the serving-girl. Though having a fit within her home with only the house staff to witness it would be far less embarrassing than what had overcome her at the party, she would still prefer to avoid any such loss of composure, if possible.

She dismissed the serving-girl and set out to solve the mystery on her own, re-examining all those corners and hidden places around their labyrinth home where the instrument may have been taken. But it was not in the entrance hall, nor the bedrooms, nor the dining room, nor the gallery, library, or even atrium—and so she had found herself stalking the back halls in a foul mood, puzzling over what may have become of it.

He wouldn't have had it destroyed or thrown out, even for her sake. He'd chosen it for her himself, and was very fond of its appearance. She didn't believe for a moment that he would have marred that perfect finish.

That left one room; the one place she had never explored in all of her idle wanderings: her husband's laboratory.

She was not allowed in there. No one was, beyond Doctor Blaubart himself. She understood why, of course. She was hardly a scientist, nor even particularly clever. It was likely that her mere presence would upset some delicate work and set him back months in his latest project. He had already given up so much of his work in his care for her that she would not usually trouble him further, but in this matter she could not deny herself.

Now with a purpose and destination in mind, she made haste towards the laboratory and, upon seeing the empty hall, immediately attempted the handle, only to find it locked tight. Of course, he wouldn't trust the servants to keep out, and so great was his love of his work that this would probably not change even after he'd replaced all their human help with his automata.

As the lady of the house, she knew where the spare key was, and only she had access to it. However, her husband had warned her to only use it in the direst of circumstances. It was not due to a lack of trust in her, of course, but instead a mere concern for her safety, or perhaps fixation upon his work; an eccentricity she had long accepted and even come to love him for.

Though this may not be the kind of emergency use her husband had envisioned when he entrusted her with that key, and perhaps he would see it as a betrayal of his trust, she could think of no other recourse.

She studied the door for a time.

He had taken from her many things in the name of her well-being. Her freedom, her interaction with society, her music … Perhaps it would seem a petty, childish thing, but to her, playing her music was a way to stake a claim to her soul. She may be diminished, but she would never be entirely snuffed out. If she could play once more, it would be all the proof she needed that she had overcome her accident and her frailty, once and for all, if only to herself.

This was the only logical place he could have hidden it, and she would get it back.

Mary slipped the key from its hiding place and carefully made her way back through the library. There was no real cause for such caution, as she was alone in the house for the first time since the idea had come to her a few weeks ago, but it made her nervous to hear her labors produce even the tiniest noise. And so she crept between the stacks back to the halls, the key clutched tight in one hand while the other held a small electric torch. The thought of lighting up whole rooms caused just as much anxiety as her fear of being heard.

Though she jumped at every shadow along the way, she soon found herself standing before the laboratory door once again. That her husband was away to a meeting, the servants sent home for the evening, and even the automata mostly disabled for core maintenance did little to calm her nerves. She took her eyes from the door to study the key. It was a peculiar thing, cylindrical and etched in strange patterns, with wires and a small red bulb on the back.

Taking a breath, she inserted it into the round keyhole and stepped back as some unseen mechanism drew the key the rest of the way into the lock and twisted it a quarter-turn with a buzz and a loud click. The red light on the rear of the key lit. She did not understand the process entirely, but knew that electricity was being directed through the key and disengaging a number of locks and other security measures around the door. Soon, there was another buzzer, and the door began to swing open on its own.

As door came fully open, the light from her electric torch revealed her piano sitting there against the far wall of the laboratory, just as she had expected. She breathed a sigh of relief as she stepped into the lab. Perhaps it would only be for a night that she could play, before she had to return everything to their proper places that her husband may not notice her disobedience. Even the promise of that one solitary night was a balm for her soul.

However, perhaps triggered by the door mechanism, lights began coming on around the room. The first thing illuminated was mere steps from her, and she shrieked as the light struck it.

It was a body.

The shock fell away somewhat, after a moment, and she realized it was not a body, but an automata, though an incredibly lifelike one. There was still something unsettling about the half-assembled device, but before she could place it, another light came on, and another. With each part of the room that lit, another project was revealed. One after another, she saw half-assembled automata appear from the dark.

The automata were ever-increasing in detail and complexity. She resumed walking through the lab, examining each one as she did. And as they progressed, that unsettling feeling returned to her, becoming a gnawing fear deep within her, as she began to understand.

As the automata became more advanced, their features became ever more familiar: more and more, each one was becoming a reflection of her own appearance.

When she saw the first one stained by dried blood, her hand flew to her mouth as she understood these automata were not abandoned in the middle of assembly, but disassembly. At some point, they had begun to be constructed with living skin that covered veins which carried real blood; blood that now stained their ruined bodies and destroyed clothing.

There must have been dozens of them in that room, ever more gruesome in their appearance as their disassembly apparently became ever more thorough to match their increasing complexity. She felt the need to retch and vomit at the sights, but nothing came.

Why? Why would he make so many duplicates of her? It had to be her husband's work. No one else could access this room, and no one else was so skilled.

Finally, with a click, a final light lit the corner of her room, near her piano, and, despite herself, she turned to look.

There, in a tall glass cylinder filled with some mysterious liquid, floated what seemed to be the most complete of the copies. It had a full face and hair, and was totally unharmed, unlike all of the others, though it had yet to be dressed. She supposed it had yet to be activated, as countless wires trailed down to the top of its head, and its eyes were open, but motionless, glassy, and dull.

Her hand went to her mouth, but she shut her eyes and turned away. She could question this later. Perhaps … perhaps she would even ask her husband. Was he somehow preparing for her inevitable death? Had he mislead her as to the severity of her condition? He wouldn't want to distress her, after all.

She took a few blind steps forward and bumped into something. Upon opening her eyes, she discovered it was her piano. A thick layer of dust covered the entire surface. Peculiar – she was certain it had been mere weeks since she'd last seen it in the drawing room. She shook her head and turned her back to the gruesome room, focusing on the keys. If she could just play one more time ….

Her fingers touched the ivory and she began one of the simplest pieces she knew. However, even playing such a childish work, and even playing more slowly than she had even when learning the instrument, her fingers seem to keep missing their marks. The motions were rough and jerky, almost like a—

A brilliant flash came from behind, and she fell to the ground, making a loud noise as she struck the piano briefly. She lay there, her body unnaturally heavy and her limbs unresponsive.

She heard heavy footsteps as her husband stepped around her prone form and placed a small device in the shape of a pistol on the worktable that stood nearby. Next to it, he sat his own key to the lab, the light on the rear of it glowing red. Not even sparing her a glance, he cleared his throat and pressed a button on the table. She heard a loud click, and he began speaking, though not to her.

"Beginning termination log, subject …" Doctor Blaubart sighed. "Damnable thing. It's been so long I've lost count. I thought I had it this time." He shook his head and continued. "Series number to be assigned later. Note to self, record over this part. Personal note, inform Lorentz that his aetheric wave design is effective in disabling zevatron-dependent devices. The antiwave canceled out the luminiferous waveform and induced catatonia instantly."

She felt him slide his arms under her own, wrapping them around her torso and lifting her unsteadily from the floor with a grunt and a muttered curse, before depositing her roughly on the worktable. She could just see the little weapon her husband had used lying beside her, and the glass cylinder holding that most advanced copy stood in the center of her vision.

"Termination of current model was due to the predicted failure point," Doctor Blaubart said, resuming monologuing to some hidden recording device. "Affixing an output modulator to the zevatron core to dull erratic emotional states and subdue the automaton produced severe power spikes that only agitated it further, and eventually lead to a cascading failure. The question of maintaining human independence and drive while still instilling necessary stability and obedience continues to elude me, though this model outlasted its predecessor by a startling margin."

She saw him placing various tools, none of which

she could identify, on the table alongside the weapon. He stopped a moment to crouch next to her and shine a bright light into her eyes, which left her desperately wanting to blink, though her body still failed to respond.

"However," the doctor continued, oblivious to or uncaring of her plight, "the timing of this failure is, in a way, fortuitous. I have recently perfected a new design which will allow the automaton much greater mobility and dexterity. As such, I will begin disassembly and inspection of joint wear shortly."

Doctor Blaubart stopped and placed the light down, turning and stepping away from his catatonic wife to place a hand on the glass cylinder.

"I'm closer to making you perfect again, darling. This time, you'll be able to play your piano."

The Mech Oni And the Three-Inch Tinkerer

Leslie and David T. Allen

Long ago in Japan, on the island of Hokkaido, there lived a tinkering couple. Though poor, they had only one desire. Every morning they walked the path between the flickering stone lanterns to the shrine on the edge of town and threw a coin in the offertory. After bowing, clapping, and ringing the large bell, they would pray:

"Please give us a child of our own. No matter how small, weak, or slow, we will love them."

Time passed, until the couple was old and grey, and after thirty years of prayer their one desire was fulfilled. True to their word, they loved their son, though he was no longer than the tip of a grown man's finger.

"We'll call him Issun Boshi," the proud new mother said with a smile. "Our three-inch son."

"Mother!" Issun called as he climbed through the grate on the small food steamer, a burnt grain of rice clutched in his hand. "This was wedged in the gears, but it should work fine now." He looked up at his mother, surprised to see a look of sorrow spreading across her face. "What's wrong?"

She sighed and gently stroked his head with her thumb. "Your place shouldn't be climbing through the guts of broken appliances, looking for problems that our old eyes can no longer see."

Issun dropped the rice and stepped forward. "I don't understand. You need my help."

"Not anymore. Thanks to you, we have enough money to retire."

"But—"

"And you're sixteen. You should be starting your own life, not tending to your parents."

"But—"

"Take a few days to consider what you want. Your father and I will do our best to help you on your way." With that, his mother turned and left.

Issun returned to the wooden box his father had made him for a room and laid on the sandal topped with a thick sock that was his bed. His friends in the village had started to make their way in the world already. Issun had always thought that, due to his small size, he would stay in the town where he was born, where his neighbors knew him, and the baker decorated special half-inch tall cakes.

None of this stoic practicality dampened his dreams. As a young boy, his parents had taken him to see a kabuki performance. Everything about it was magnificent, but the strutting samurai character captivated him. Issun had idled away hours wearing a thimble as a helmet and swinging a pine needle, imagining he was the hero with the katana.

The next morning, he woke to the early summer sun and entered the kitchen where his parents were having tea.

"I want to be a samurai," he said.

His parents sat in silence for a moment before his father nodded. "Just because you're small doesn't mean you cannot be mighty."

His mother smiled. "Though you may not be a samurai in title, all it takes is strength, honor, and bravery to be a samurai in deed. You've proven yourself more than capable of that. We'll need a few days to prepare your things."

Though sad to leave his parents, Issun could hardly wait. Three days later he woke and entered the kitchen to find several ornate boxes waiting for him.

In the first he found a long, steel sewing needle, the eye a perfect width to use as a handle. In the second he found a 500 yen coin, wrapped in wire with a handle on the back.

"Your sword and shield," his mother said.

The last box was so large that his father had to help him open it. Inside was a fine tea-bowl and two chopsticks.

"And your ship, to carry you to adventure," his father said, his voice gruff with emotion.

Issun saw the tears in their eyes. "My own ship,

so I can go and come back."

He had meant for his warm words to comfort their hearts, but their frowns only deepened.

"The current is strong, son. You'll find travelling upstream impossible."

Setting his jaw, Issun stormed to their workshop. "I won't leave like that."

For three days he worked in secret, only to emerge on the fourth with a broad smile. "Come look!" he called, waving for his parents to follow.

Flanking the bowl were two small turbine-like wheels that attached to a mechanical fan. "See?" Issun laughed. "The current is strong, which will let this fan power the engine."

His parents smiled and told him how clever he was, and the moment was so full of joy he thought his heart might burst. They shared one last breakfast together, reminiscing about the past and making excited guesses about the future, until his mother laid her hand on the table. "It's time, son."

Issun stepped onto her palm, then was gently placed in the tea bowl and carried outside. The townspeople had gathered around the river, waving banners, ready to send him off.

"This river will take you to Sapporo," his father said as he lowered Issun's bowl into the gently moving waters. "Take care, son."

"Ganbatte!" the townspeople yelled, wishing him luck.

Issun navigated the river, using his chopsticks as oars. He peered out when passing villages, keeping an eye out for the Sapporo skyline he'd memorized from staring at a woodblock print hanging in his parents' home.

Soon the surge of the river gave way to the sounds of steam and stone, and the forests thinned to reveal the brick factories that made the appliances he had spent his life repairing. The waters became choppy as steamboats docked and unloaded passengers and goods.

Issun, worried about the traffic near the dock, steered further downstream before turning toward the riverbank. With the edge of his little boat touching land, he climbed over the side, but quickly realized he lacked the strength to pull it from the water.

"Maybe someone will help me," he muttered, looking around for a friendly face, but the only people nearby swarmed the docks. The shuffling of feet, the churning of wheels, and the spray of water made him think twice about approaching. It would be too easy to be squished.

With a sigh, he sat at the edge of the river. His adventure had barely begun, and he'd already made a mistake. How would he ever get home? Watching the water, he waited for inspiration to strike, but instead his attention was turned to a bit of rope that was anchored to the ground and stretched into the water.

He frowned. It had to be a trap. He hated them, having once been caught in one himself. Grabbing his sword from the boat, he stormed over to the rope—which was thicker than his arm—and began hacking away. It took a few minutes, but eventually each fiber split, and the rope disappeared into the water.

"Be safe, fishies!" Issun cried, before realizing that had been his first act as a samurai. Embarrassed, he instead struck a pose and nodded solemnly.

A luminescent white splotch—unearthly bright, especially from underwater—moved toward him.

Trying to control the hammering in his chest, he waited with his sword at the ready. Perhaps the trap hadn't been without merit.

Two bulbous eyes emerged from the water, followed by a flat head and a wide mouth. A flash of terror surged through Issun: he rarely saw frogs that big. To it, he might look like a tasty snack.

Unwilling to abandon his vessel, he raised his katana. "Go away!"

One of the great white frog's eyes blinked, followed a half-second later by the other. "Have you no request of me, little one?"

Issun half-lowered his weapon. "Huh?"

"You have rescued a river-spirit; it is only fitting that I return the favor."

"Oh." Issun scratched his chin. "Could you help me with my boat?"

The spirit-frog turned to look at the tea bowl, but remained silent.

"I'll need it later, but I don't know where to keep it safe."

"I know of such a place. When you need your vessel, return anywhere along this riverbank and call my name: Suijin. But be careful of the forest; I have spotted from the banks a steam-warrior possessed by an oni, and he loathes trespassers in his domain." The spirit-frog extended a large, webbed hand.

Issun retrieved his shield and sack. Awestruck, he watched the frog disappear downstream. Not even a day into his journey of being a samurai, and he had saved a river-spirit.

Feeling confident, he turned and headed away from the busy docks, then walked inland. Dodging feet, wheels, kicked stones, and the occasional dog left him panting by the time he found a small park. He rested beneath a bench, where he ate the seaweed-wrapped rice grains his mother had packed for him.

His brief respite was interrupted by the attention of a girl—perhaps his age, but normal-sized—dressed in a red shibori kimono.

"Hello," she said, sitting on her knees. Issun stood up and struck a pose, using his 500 yen coin shield and sewing needle katana. The girl giggled and clapped.

"I'm Yuki Suenaga," she said, pointing at her nose.

"Suenaga of Suenaga Industries?" Issun asked. He had seen that name a thousand times, stamped on the numerous appliances he had repaired.

Yuki nodded, confirming she was a daimyo princess. "Who are you, tiny warrior?"

Issun sheathed his sewing needle. A god and a princess in one day. His would be the best samurai story of them all. "I am Issun Boshi, and I'm seeking a samurai apprenticeship."

Yuki tilted her head as she considered this. "I can take you to see my father, young ronin."

Issun rode on her shoulder, standing with a hand on his hilt, imitating a stance he thought was befitting of a samurai. Yuki entered a brick building in the Suenaga factory complex. Issun inhaled the scent of linseed oil and traced the root-like system of pneumatic tubes, in which messages were flying every which way.

Yuki passed the secretary and burst into a rococo office, the interior of which was finer than any Issun had ever seen. A man sat behind a large desk, wearing a black suit.

"Father, I've found a little ronin!" she said, interrupting him as he spoke into a brass horn.

"It's my daughter; we'll have to speak later." Mr. Suenaga flipped a switch then stood. "Yuki-chan, what are you talking about?"

Yuki gestured at her shoulder. "See, father?"

Mr. Suenaga took a closer look at Issun, who was standing as still as a statue. "Where did you find such a doll?"

Issun bowed, startling the daimyo, and then spoke. "Suenaga-sama, I am Issun Boshi. I hail from a small village north of Sapporo. I'm in search of a master, so that I can train to become a samurai. I have already rescued a river-spirit, and I know even greater trials and successes await me."

Mr. Suenaga put his monocle in place and took a closer look. "I've never seen anything like this before. You say you're from up north … are you a Koropok-guru?"

It was not the first time that Issun had been compared to the tiny people in Ainu mythology. The difference was, they were a myth; he was real.

"No, I am Japanese."

"Fascinating." Mr. Suenaga stroked the graying stubble at his chin. "I don't know that we have a position for a samurai right now."

"Father …." Yuki pleaded, warming her father's heart.

A warm heart was not enough, though—business is business. Mr. Suenaga considered how little space the three-inch-high samurai would require, and how little he would eat. "My daughter has a way of finding herself in trouble; she could use a guardian. Yes, Issun Boshi, I will accept your service, but your rent and food will come out of your salary."

Yuki hugged her father, putting Issun awkwardly close to the man; he merely held his samurai stance. She skipped away, leaving Issun to fall, clinging to her shoulder.

Issun woke early, every morning, to train in the sunlight streaming through Yuki's bedroom window while she slept. To improve his technique, Yuki took Issun to borrow samurai books from the library. He walked across the sentences as he read about techniques and history.

His life was not all exercise and studying. Yuki was a playful girl who loved him dearly. One time, with his permission, she placed him in a capsule and sent him zipping through the pneumatic message tubes. Issun, unaccustomed to travelling at such speeds, got sick inside the capsule. Their adventures became tamer after that.

Issun did his best to describe his experiences. Yuki was always curious about how he saw the world, and he was happy to have someone close to his age to talk to.

As the shortening days hinted at winter, Yuki fancied a walk. Issun, happy to follow Yuki's lead, sat on her shoulder as she boarded a train. It wasn't until she descended the steps at the next station, her path leading them perilously close to the forest, that Issun realized her destination and recalled the river-spirit's warning.

"We shouldn't go into the woods," he said solemnly. "It's not safe."

"That's why I have you," Yuki replied with a laugh.

Issun frowned but didn't respond. They walked,

her chattering about the fresh smell of the woods, the beauty of the leaves, and the pleasing sound of the stream, while he remained silent.

The chirping of cicadas hushed suddenly, and Issun's budding samurai instincts surged. Gripping the eye of his needle, he leaned forward. "Something is wrong."

The trees rustled, shuddering at the banshee screech of hydraulics. Above the woods rose a cloud of smog. A high pitch whir accompanied the spinning sawmill blade cutting through the dense foliage, exposing the sight of a monster that looked more like the demons he'd seen in wood-block prints than a mechanical warrior.

Two eerie, green eyes glowed from this monster's lumpy iron face. Just above each painted eyebrow was a short, golden goat horn. From ear to ear spanned the jaw, filled with serrated silver teeth and boar-like tusks. The red body paint had scraped off in places, and the shoulders were dented from knocking down trees. One clawed hand was clutching a marble club; the other arm ended in the saw blade. About its waist was a shiny tiger-print iron loin cloth, which moved like platemail.

"What-Have-We-Here?" emitted its voice.

Issun could feel Yuki trembling. How small she looked, compared to this monstrosity! Issun, who was accustomed to looking up at everyone, was less intimidated. Holding his sword and shield in position, he puffed out his chest. "I am the samurai Issun Boshi!"

The mech's telescopic eyes zoomed in. It laid down the marble club to hold its clawed hand to its brows to block out the sunlight streaming through the canopy. "Who-Said-That?"

Issun scaled down Yuki's body and stepped before her, flashing his sewing needle katana. "It was me: Issun Boshi!"

"Ha-Ha-Ha," came the single pitched laugh, followed by the sound of a dozen tiny motors sculpting its face into a sneer. "I-Had-Not-Seen-You-Little … Samurai!"

Issun had not been laughed at since he was two inches tall, when the other kids were still callous and ignorant. His knuckles whitened as he gripped the needle's eye.

The iron creature stooped down to reclaim its club. "You-Are-In-My-Domain! What-Gift-Have-You-Brought-Me?"

Issun steeled himself. "You deserve nothing, lump face!"

The saw blade whirred, and the telescopic eyes twisted to refocus. "Then-The-Girl-Will-Be-My-Prisoner-And-You-Will-Be-Crushed!"

Issun dashed forward. The saw arm came down, cleaving tree roots where he had been just a second before. The mech raised a clawed foot and stomped, narrowly missing Issun, but providing him purchase to climb.

It lifted its leg and bent down, searching to see if it had squashed the little samurai. Taking the opportunity of the monster being unbalanced, Yuki ran forward to knock it down, but its mass was too much for the hundred-and-twenty pound girl. The mech smacked her aside with its club.

"Yuki!" Issun cried, though even in his fear he refused to give up. Heaving his katana over his head, he slammed it into the hip joint. The iron giant dropped the club and, using his claws, picked Issun up by the collar of his shirt. He just managed to grab his sword before being dangled above its stiff, smiling face.

Issun's heart dropped at the clicking sound accompanying the opening mouth beneath him. He kicked and squirmed, freeing himself from his shirt before the jaw was ready to close.

Darkness enclosed him as he fell through the mechanical throat onto a rotating cog. His shield clattered from his arm and fell into dark guts of the demon. Disoriented, Issun sat, spinning, while his eyes adjusted to what little light that entered the pinpoint gaps through the metal skin.

The interior was far more complicated than anything Issun had ever repaired, but some parts were familiar. He lost his balance as the platform lurched; the mech was walking.

"Where-Are-You-Girl?"

"Yuki!" Issun's shout echoed. The cogs continued to spin and, remembering that burnt grain of rice that had broken the entire food steamer, he drove his needle into the intersecting teeth. The mechanics came to a halt, for a short time, until the force was too great and the needle snapped.

As the mechanics resumed, Issun frantically crawled through the steel guts, seeking something to wedge between the gears. Light reflected off a familiar shape: his shield! Issun scrambled toward it, hugged the coin to his chest, and began climbing. The mech lurched, breaking Issun's grasp and again he fell. Spots danced before his eyes, but he still clutched the coin.

When his vision cleared, he spotted another set

of gears only a few inches above him. He carefully climbed the mechanics and, bracing himself, fit the coin between the teeth of the gears.

For a moment nothing happened, until the demon shook and a horrible screech grew and Issun had to cover his ears. Then the mech, and Issun with it, was falling, and in the darkened chaos all he could do was cover his head and pray.

When the demon finally lay still, Issun braved a look around. A circle of light shone and he carefully picked through the broken machine. Once he reached the mouth, he stepped into the grass and looked around.

Aside from Yuki's discarded kimono, he saw nothing but the devastation the monster had caused. "Yuki!" he called, running to her dress. It was torn, and a smear of blood shone sticky near the shoulder. Tears formed in the corners of his eyes, and a sob escaped him.

"What troubles you, little one?"

Issun turned to see a painfully bright-white fox trotting toward him.

"You can bring her back, right?" Issun swallowed a gulp. Samurais didn't cry.

The fox's brow arched as if confused.

"Issun?" came a small voice. A bump in the fabric shifted.

"Yuki?" he cried, charging across the kimono to the voice.

Her tiny head and the top of her bare shoulders—one stained with blood—popped through a tear in the fabric. "What happened?"

The spirit-fox flicked its tail. "That was no ordinary club that struck you, Yuki Suenaga," the spirit-fox said. "That was Uchide's club. It can shrink and enlarge whatever it strikes."

Yuki peeked under the fabric and looked down at her body. A smile slowly formed on her face. "Issun, I'm your size!"

"A ... a bit shorter, I think," Issun said, uncomfortable but not displeased with her exposure.

"Give me a second," Yuki said, clutching a section of the oversized kimono around her body. "Um ... Issun ... can you turn around? You too, fox."

Issun and the fox did as she asked. Issun heard fabric ripping behind him.

"Ready!" she called.

Issun turned to see her standing, two-and-a-half inches tall, in a makeshift kimono.

She was beaming. "We can have so much fun! I always wondered what it was like, rocketing through the pneumatic tubes!"

Issun's stomach tightened. "I ... I guess we could try that again. But it's going to take a while to get back to the train, given we're lost and neither of us is ... tall." Issun frowned up at the fox. "Could you give us a ride back to the train station?"

The fox shook his great head. "My power is limited to the forest."

Issun remembered the frog he had saved months earlier. "What about the river? Could you take us there?"

The fox smiled a foxy smile. "If that is your wish. You've done us a great service by ridding the woods of the fabricated oni."

Issun smiled and turned to Yuki, taking her hands in his own. "How would you like to meet my parents?"

"I'd love to." Yuki's smile matched his own, and with the beginning of a blush already forming, she leaned in and kissed him on the cheek.

Together, they rode on the fox's back to the bank of the river, where Issun called for Suijin. The frog emerged from the water, along with a large bubble. Inside the bubble was Issun's tea-bowl boat. The bubble popped, and the bowl was perfectly dry.

Issun lent Yuki a hand, then hopped in himself. He kicked on the motors, which were powerful enough to overcome the river's current. Issun and Yuki looked back, holding hands, and waved to Suijin and the fox-god.

The Copper Eyes

Allison Latzko

Oliver was certain his mother was up to something horrid when his brothers disappeared into her workshop, a room no one ever entered.

His mother—a brilliant inventor—had been acting peculiar for days, and as the evening lengthened and his older brothers helped their mother, Oliver's curiosity grew. He waited outside with thinning patience as metal clanked and gears rattled in the other room. Plans and blueprints of mechanisms and engines crowded every nook and cranny of their cottage home, and on those pages existed complex and brilliant designs. Oliver picked up a draft, running his thumb along the page before he set it down, wishing others could see the genius his mother was. Heaps of ideas and designs remained incomplete, and even more had been stolen from her, patented by other more recognized inventors.

The clock above him chimed and Oliver realized it was almost midnight. Too much time had passed; his patience had expired.

He crept up to the workshop door. A lock kept him out, but he was used to picking it from many times before. He nudged the door open and peered into the large room. Inventions occupied the floors and shelves and in the center of the room sat his mother's worktable, covered in contraptions—his family was nowhere in sight. He stepped to the table, picked up a pair of leather goggles, and examined them. Gold framed the amber lenses. His mother always wore them while she worked; she never finished anything without them.

A buzzing noise went off, and Oliver's head snapped up. He hid the goggles behind his back. On the opposite side of the room, two long tables stretched out with hunks of iron lying on top. Oliver moved closer. The inventions were shaped like animals made of metal, gears and bolts; one in the shape of a dog, the other an eagle. Both were a human length, and their orange glassy eyes stared up aimlessly, the sight of them stalling Oliver's heart.

"Oliver, what are you doing here?" his mother asked, and then he saw her. She stood against the wall, her fingers twisting around a long flat tool in her hand.

"What are you working on?" he asked.

"You always need to know, don't you?"

She smiled, but Oliver sensed something darker

in that look. He'd seen it quite often when she noticed him or his brothers observing her work.

"So curious," she added. "I had to stop it."

"What do you mean?" he asked. "Where are my brothers?"

Her eyes trailed to the machines, and Oliver's blood went cold as he realized what she'd done. The metal machines – though animalistic – were also familiar.

"No one will steal my inventions anymore. Not even my sons."

His mother pulled a lever down on the wall beside her; the orange eyes of the two metal animals blazed like fire and they rose from their tables like Frankenstein's creation, metal scraping the tables.

Oliver turned, sprinted from the room and raced out of the house. The doors slammed behind him as he gasped for breath. In the cottage he heard projects smashing into the ground and his mother's voice growing louder.

"Oliver, come back," she called through the door. The words ran off her tongue like venom. "You can't just leave."

He scrambled away from the house and down the hill, never once looking back. He ran as far as he could, over rocks and fallen branches, to the only place he could think of.

The nearby village glowed before him like a beacon of hope. When he made it to the square, he exhaled in relief. The sounds of squeaking gears and grinding were gone, but above him a winged creature drifted through the sky and the tree line danced as something pushed against the branches.

He leaned against a wall as he trembled,

imagining his brothers, whom he'd always been so close to, descending upon him with a remorseless force. As the minutes passed, his heartbeat slowed. For now he knew he was safe.

Oliver moved to wipe his tear-stained face. Only then did he realize what he still had, and he gazed at them in wonder. In his fingers were his mother's copper goggles, shining brilliantly in the moonlight.

Guests bustled through the small inn, drinking and laughing as the innkeeper shuffled around with their meals. Lantern light illuminated the pub, giving it a pleasant feel amidst the grimy tables and dirty crowd.

Oliver sat at one of the tables as the innkeeper set a plate of stew and potatoes in front of him. Heat drifted off the food and his stomach rumbled. Warmth spread from his stomach as he ate.

"—t's 'ery good," Oliver said to the innkeeper through a mouthful of stew.

The old woman laughed and patted him on the shoulder. "I'm glad you like it."

Oliver had grown accustomed to the familiar faces at the inn. It had been two weeks and the nightmare of what he'd seen in his mother's workshop had not abated, but the familiar drone of the inn, the crowds and cheerful banter had almost doused his fear. The innkeeper had taken him in in exchange for his assistance with chores, and he'd been more than grateful. Most nights it was a peaceful reprieve and a nice distraction. Even so, he knew he could not return home.

As the evening wore on, the door of the inn slammed open and three men entered. Their chairs scraped across the wooden floor; their voices loud and hysteric. The innkeeper sighed in annoyance, snapping her rag, and moved to greet her newest customers. Oliver regarded them, swinging his feet under the chair as they spoke, their frightened tones swept through the room.

"—not going to be safe for long. The stairs are gone and the place will crash down at any moment."

"We almost died! It was the beast's fault!" The man held out his arms to describe something rather large. At first, the mechanic creatures had been nothing more than a remarkable sight in the village. But Oliver could tell from the men's expressions that something had transpired, and a rush of fear gripped his chest. He listened in. They had been at the clock tower waiting to see the beasts. At midnight, they'd appeared; one a giant metal bird with iron wings, swooping and twisting in the air; the other a massive canine that pounded its way through the village woods, its gears groaning and creaking. Then they attacked the villagers with claws and teeth. A boy with them had gotten hurt.

"And that stupid girl!" the one man said. "She hid up in the tower. We tried to get her out but it's impossible."

Oliver's eyes widened. The men's voices quieted, and Oliver hopped off the chair, ducking under the table nearest them.

"How long has she been up there?" one of them asked.

"Two days. Dumb girl's probably frightened out of her mind."

"Hopefully, the monsters disappear so we can get to her."

"We'll be lucky the tower doesn't topple before that."

Oliver's hands turned to fists and he closed his eyes, taking a deep breath. "Excuse me," he said, popping up and alerting the men. They stared at him with open mouths. "Where is she trapped?" he asked.

"The old clock tower," one said, dumbstruck.

"Thank you." Oliver nodded and raced out the door, ignoring their calls to return.

The old clock tower loomed over the edge of town. The ancient brass hands progressed steadily as Oliver crept up to it, gazing up at it in wonder. He was surprised the clock still functioned properly, considering the wreckage the metal beast had caused. It looked as though the building would tip over any moment, back into the woods where nature could finally reclaim it.

Fear ran rampant through his heart. His legs felt like jelly, and he had the urge to run back into the village and continue hiding at the inn. But he knew he had to remedy the chaos his mother had begun. The creatures were looking for him, after all, and he'd done nothing but hide. Now a girl's life was involved.

The clock sounded eleven times, leaving only an hour until the beasts appeared. He could make it up there in time, if he tried.

Setting his lantern down, he grabbed the amber goggles resting on his head and placed the large lenses over his eyes. As soon as he did, a whizzing noise picked up, steam blew off above his head, and suddenly the glass inside the goggles changed, illuminating his way with green symbols and instructions.

Bits of debris covered the ground and walls of the floor of the tower. Nothing remained of the staircase that had existed to his left, and there were still two levels above. The goggles pinpointed an object in sight with an emerald arrow. If he shoved the fallen wooden beam to the right two feet three inches, he could secure what remained of the stairs above. Then he had to move the rubbish and use a stack of crates to reach the rest of the stairs.

Smiling, Oliver pushed the wooden beam as the goggles instructed. It moved easily. He tossed bits of wood and metal out of his way and stacked the crates until they were sturdy enough to climb. When he got to solid ground on the second level, the remainder of the stairwell rested before him. He stepped lightly onto the first quivering step. Then he gripped the railing on both sides and ventured up.

The clock ticked much louder at the top of the tower. He stepped off the stairs and saw the darkened village through the face of the clock, covering everything in an amber film. On the floor lay scattered pieces of metal and wires. Two miniature bronze boxes sat in the center with large knobs and rusty silver claws attached. A thin wire linked them.

Hunched over those boxes sat the girl he'd come to rescue.

Golden strands of hair fell down around her ears and the rest was haphazardly tied back. Her red dress was covered in dirt and dust, but she didn't seem to care, gazing down at her contraption with every bit of concentration.

"Hello?" Oliver asked, and the girl's head shot up. Her mouth dropped open.

"Stop! Don't move!" she shouted, holding out her hand. Oliver paused mid-step.

"Who are you?" she asked. "What are you doing here?"

"I'm the rescue party, of course."

She scrutinized him with narrowed eyes. Oliver raised his foot but the girl held up both hands.

"I said stop moving! You need to be careful!"

He glanced at the floor. A green line ran across the lenses of the goggles, directing his safe passage, but Oliver didn't know what the girl was capable of, so he remained still.

Anger and curiosity flitted across her face. "You look odd, like an automaton. Take off those glasses so I can see you."

The room darkened significantly as he pulled the goggles off, and he noticed a small bout of light from the girl's lantern on the floor.

"You're practically working in the dark!"

She tilted her head. "My father would have never sent a grimy boy like you. What's your name?"

"Oliver. You?"

"Aileen." She rose from her spot. Specks of dirt hung in the air as she tiptoed forward to give him a better look. "Aileen Codges. How'd you find the entrance?"

"A bit of luck and some magic."

She scoffed. "Luck sounds about right."

For just a moment, Oliver considered walking out the door. His own eyes narrowed. "Everyone in town is worried about you."

"I don't need saving." She crossed her arms. "I could have easily made my way downstairs. I hid the entryway on purpose."

"You hid it? Why?"

"It doesn't matter." She waved her arms. "You can go back and tell everyone I'm perfectly fine. They don't need to worry."

His eyes lingered over her project. As crude as it was, he wanted badly to know what it was. "What are you doing up here?"

"Saving the town. Stopping the monsters." A spark shot from the metal box, causing Aileen to cry and wince. "Darn it!"

Oliver raised an eyebrow. "It looks like you may need help."

"I'm perfectly fine. Please go back now. Step lightly."

He held out his goggles, and Aileen paused. "I know an unfinished project when I see one, and according to what I've heard, you've already been here two days. The goggles can help you finish it."

She hesitated, biting her lip, but Oliver felt her resolve cracking. "Why should I trust you?"

"Why wouldn't you trust your rescue party?" Then he added, more seriously, "A boy was hurt. I want to help stop them before it gets out of hand."

She leaned over and grabbed his goggles, placing them over her own eyes, the strap bunching up her hair and the lenses giving her an alien look. As soon as they were on, the gears in the glasses hummed, puffing out more smoke. Her mouth opened in awe, and she looked around.

"These are magnificent! Where did you find them?" All the menace in her voice had vanished. A smile lit her dirty face.

"They're mine."

She plopped herself on the wooden floor—her

dress sending even more dust into the air—and grabbed one of the metal boxes along with a small wrench. "Those beasts outside the village. They're on a timer if you haven't noticed. Midnight is when they'll arrive for an hour doing who knows what. There has to be a way to stop them, and I believe I can make their internal clock stop."

"And how do you plan on doing that?"

"By short-circuiting them." Her fingers moved quickly, threading wires and screwing bolts into place. She held up one of her bronze boxes. "I've created this with the things I've found. We'll have to connect it to the monsters, unfortunately, but once that's done it'll shut them down. These goggles will help me finish it in no time."

"You're quite good," Oliver said, watching with interest. "Doing all of that on your own."

Aileen shrugged. "Thanks. Although I doubt I'm as great as the person who owned these goggles. They must have invented some marvelous things."

The rumbling from outside grew louder and she paused. Oliver kneeled in the doorway and watched. Aileen worked diligently, only stopping to switch tools.

"So where did you steal these?" she asked, tapping the lens. "You couldn't have made them. In fact, I don't think anyone could have. They're too perfect."

"I didn't steal them," he muttered. "I borrowed them."

Aileen's mouth formed a thin line. "Sounds like stealing to me."

He frowned and was about to reply when the clock struck twelve. The building shook, consuming every other sound.

"Oh no."

He glanced at the window. A shadow passed and a darkened creature rushed down in the moonlight. Terror built in his chest.

"We're out of time."

Aileen's goggled eyes looked down as she twisted a screw into her box. "I have to finish this."

"We have to go. If it hits the tower—"

"But I'm not finished!"

"Finish it on the way down."

He rushed forward and grabbed Aileen, pulling her up. They ran. Aileen led them out and down the stairs, Oliver following blindly until they reached his stack of crates. The lantern he'd left behind illuminated the ground as they climbed down.

When the final chime struck, they tumbled out the door. The winged creature made its final attack on the building, diving into the tower like a torpedo. Seconds later the tower smashed into the woods with a loud crash, taking trees down like a line of dominoes.

The creature rose again and circled above. Then it dived. Oliver pulled Aileen and himself out of the way, and they tumbled into the grass. Aileen toyed with the screw and the boxes in her hand, her head still bent down.

"Aileen, we have to go!" Oliver cried in between breaths. He grabbed her arm and tried to wrench her away but she refused to move.

"It's finished!" She held up her device. "We need to attach it to its back!"

They looked up just in time to see the creature. Aileen waited patiently, staring it down. It lunged again, missing her by inches, and she threw her device.

They heard a loud thump as metal claws pierced the beast. Cheering, Aileen pressed down on the button of the box she still held. Electricity surged through her device, through the wires and into the claws attached to the beast. The machine's gears halted. The beast juddered and hit the ground with a large thud.

A grin spread across Aileen's face as she tore the goggles off and jumped up. "We did it! These goggles are brilliant!"

Oliver raced over to the machine, falling beside it. He seized bits of bronze and iron sheets covering the creature and pulled at them. Aileen kneeled beside him to help, unscrewing bolts with her wrench. She pulled at a wing and fell back with a start as the piece she tore off revealed a human hand.

"Is that—" Aileen began, eyes wide as she leaned back.

"He's my brother."

They disassembled the beast until only his brother remained, his eyes closed and skin pale. Oliver felt his breath on his hand and sighed in relief.

"How did this happen?" Aileen asked, observing Oliver's brother and the scattered pieces in astonishment. She gritted her teeth.

"My mother ... she used those goggles to invent the creatures." He gazed down and closed his eyes. "She did this."

"Why would she do something like this? To her own sons?"

Oliver shoulders sagged. "She was afraid." He took a deep breath. "I'm sorry. I should have done something or told someone about them."

Aileen stepped closer. She held out her hand and smiled at him, warming his heart. "It's okay, Oliver. We stopped them in time."

The trees rustled, and they both looked up. Two amber globes burned before them in the darkened woods.

"We only stopped one," he said, slowly rising. "The other one. It's here."

Aileen took his hand and squeezed it. Her gaze was steely. "Let's stop this one too." She handed Oliver the goggles and her own device. "It's all yours."

He placed the goggles over his eyes. The fog cleared, and the lenses told him what he needed to do.

Aileen moved the unconscious boy out of the way as the second creature stumbled out of the woods on its thick legs. Its bronze nails dug into the muddy ground. Steam rolled out of an iron snout with every husky breath it took, and it stared Oliver down with blazing eyes.

He waited as instructed. The large creature pounded closer. Then it charged. He chucked the wired device at the creature and ducked out of its path. To his surprise, the metal connected with a clink, and the claws pierced the beast. He pressed the switch. The machine halted in its tracks, smacking the junk-covered ground with a great crash, spurting up even more dirt and spare parts. Smoke flowed from its engine as the gears cooled down.

Like the first, Oliver and Aileen tore it to pieces until nothing remained except a pile of junk and his other brother, unconscious and thin, yet unharmed.

When they finally finished, their hands and faces were covered in grease and dirt. Aileen wiped her forehead with the back of her hand. Oliver smiled in relief. A quiet night had settled around them and Oliver recognized the sound of the clock tower, still ticking even though it had crashed.

Pulling off the goggles, he held them out for Aileen to take. "For you. And everything you did."

She shook her head, grinning. "They're yours, Oliver. You keep them. Besides, I think you'll need them."

His brothers awoke and Oliver told them what happened, and who saved them. The town spoke about the beasts for weeks, but there was no mention of Aileen Codges, the miller's daughter, who disappeared into the background just like the fallen clock tower.

Town saved and chaos averted, Oliver had one last thing to do.

When the bell rang and the inventor opened her door, her three sons stood before her. She looked at them from within her cottage, where her inventions had remained untouched. Revulsion filled her eyes. Oliver and his brothers knew there was no love remaining in their mother's heart; something evil had taken root there.

Her eyes locked on the goggles resting on Oliver's head. She lunged at him, shouting, but his brothers held her back. Oliver clutched Aileen's shiny new device, then tossed it into her home. Wires sprung out of the device and clawed ends connected to the metal husks in every room. He pressed his switch, and the inventions it had attached to fizzed to life, sparking and whirring until they sputtered out and became nothing but junk.

Inventions destroyed, his mother raced over to them, her screams echoing through her home and her curses hanging in the air. "Monsters," she muttered, over and over again. "Taking my goggles. Stealing my work like I knew you would! Just like everyone else!"

His brothers moved to confront her, but Oliver held them back. "Let's go. The town folk can deal with her." He glanced across the dusty room, a thin smile cresting his face. He tapped the lens of the goggles. "Besides, she's harmless now."

The brothers left, hearts weighing greatly in their chests. But they were alive, and they were safe, and Oliver knew that was all that mattered. He gripped Aileen's device in his hand, set the goggles over his eyes, and let them light the way.

Strawberry

Sins

Heather White

He gingerly held the flask up to the light. The chartreuse liquid inside bubbled and smoked, the caustic scent burning his nostrils, but the solution appeared stable. He breathed in hard to ease the tightness of his chest. Had he done it?

He tapped the glass with a clawed nail. Too hard. The liquid sloshed up the side and flashed, settling back down in a gooey brown mess.

He roared and flung the flask across the room. It shattered on the other side of his lab, a brown smear slipping down the wall. Slumping into his seat, he buried his face in his paws. Was this what he was reduced to? He, Dr. Samuel Wolfe, the man who had brought the Parisian army to its knees with his Cold Induced Temporal Arrestor.

The notes made no sense, even the parts that

weren't encoded! *How* had Fermin changed the formula? Wolfe's half of the serum had been right. Obviously, given his current form. Step one to an indomitable force, to the super soldier. But Fermin's part! The control! It was warped. And Wolfe's mind! His mind was … was …

A knock interrupted his musings.

He lumbered up the stairs from the basement and into the foyer. Another solicitor. They had been coming by every day since Fermin had been locked away. Damnable fools. As if they didn't know. Well, two could play at the charade.

"Doctor Fermin and I are under quarantine!" Wolfe coughed into his paw, a hacking sound that rumbled into a growl. Damn. The effects of the potion were accelerating more rapidly than expected. "You will have to return another time!"

"Doctor Wolfe?" a woman's voice called from beyond the door. "My name is Eliza Fermin. Doctor Fermin's daughter."

"His … daughter?" Did Fermin have a daughter? The old man had mentioned something before he was incarcerated. What had it been? Had it been that his daughter was coming to visit?

That fool just *had* to go shooting his mouth off at the club, hadn't he? In Inspector Grant's presence no less. To think Wolfe's last human days had been spent ensuring Fermin was placed in an asylum instead of jail!

"Correct. May I come in?" the woman replied.

Lights. He had to kill the lights. And close the curtains. Then let her in, tell her what happened to her father, and get her on her way. "One … one moment please."

The foyer was properly shaded when he undid the locks and cracked the door open for her, allowing him to retreat back into the shadows. A slim young woman stepped into the hall, the light streaming in behind her. She wore a heavy motoring dress, with a scarf and flap cap covering her blonde hair. A pair of goggles were perched above the brim of her cap.

Setting down a small bag, she pulled off her heavy canvas gloves. "Invigorating day for driving, don't you think? The new aether engines are much smoother than their predecessors."

"I would not know, madam. Driving has never been a hobby of mine."

"Ah, well, you'll just have to take my word for it then. Now, I have a bag here and a few things in my car that need to be brought in, if you'd be so kind …."

Wolfe cleared his throat. "My apologies, but I must be blunt. I don't know what your intent here is, but if it's to visit your father, I am afraid that—"

"He's been locked up? Oh, that's old news." She waved her hand dismissively.

He frowned. How had she known that? He had made sure to keep it out of the papers, and he was sure the solicitors came because Grant was looking for an excuse to raid the premises. "Then I am sure you understand that I must ask you to leave. The impropriety of—"

"Is this not my father's house? If anything, I should ask you to leave. There was an inspector who was quite surprised I would be heading this way. He seemed highly interested in the goings-on here." She smiled in his direction, her lips tight, teeth showing. The fur on the back of his neck rose. But then she laughed. "I wouldn't do that though. There's work to be done, isn't there?"

What sort of woman laughed off a threat like that? "Madame, I am not at liberty to say. If you can come back when your father has been released, then I am certain that—"

"You are hedging, good sir. I despise that." She slapped her gloves in her palm before smiling again. "But I know all about my father's work. In fact, let me see you. In the light. We mustn't skulk about in the dark."

"Madam, I—" He'd frighten her, and then all *would* be lost as Inspector Grant would have his excuse to come rushing in.

"Please?" She tilted her head and held out a hand, imploringly.

He breathed in deeply, taking in her scent. What was that perfume she was wearing? Fruity with a hint of something tantalizingly musky …. No! He should force her out. Deny her request and make her leave. He breathed in again. Strawberries. That's what he was smelling. But what was the harm? She was Fermin's daughter. Perhaps she'd have a key to fixing her father's mess among her belongings. Or know where to look among Fermin's.

He stepped out into the light.

She gasped and covered her mouth. Wolfe restrained a wince. He could only imagine how he looked in her eyes, towering over her, his body covered in fur, the muzzle full of teeth jutting out, the pointed ears and claws. Fortunately his dignity was spared thanks to a large pair of pants and a now torn lab coat.

"You mean … you really did it? You and my

father—?" Her mouth opened into the shape of an O before she clapped her hands. "How wonderful!"

"Wonderful? As a first step, I suppose, but the formula was flawed. Your father's half failed, and now I can't reverse the effects!" He slammed his fist against the wall, leaving a cracked indentation. He took a deep breath and let it out slowly. "Apologies. Since the transformation, I find it hard to control myself at times."

"Oh, don't apologize to me. I should be apologizing for my father. He never could follow through." She stepped closer and touched his muzzle, guiding it gently this way and that as she looked him over. "It is an *amazing* transformation though. Your work?"

He should step back. But it had been years since a woman touched him. "Yes, madam. Some of my best."

"Undoubtedly. Which is why we must fix it!"

"Fix it?" He chuckled, the laugh rumbling through his chest like a purr. "Reversing your father's formula and correcting it is what I aim to do. Which is more reason why you must leave. It is simply too dangerous for a young woman to remain here, with me!"

"Can you read them?"

"Read them?" He frowned.

She crossed her arms. "My father's notes. Can you read them?"

"Well, no, but--"

"Fortunately for you, my father taught me his work and his cipher." Taking a small step toward him, she slowly put her hand on his arm. "Please. Let me help. With my father confined, this is an opportunity for me to correct his work! An opportunity to put it to a greater use!"

Wolfe looked down at her and then at the sunlit street framed by the open door. A small silver two-seater was parked out on the lane, its aether crystal still unhooded and warming in the sunlight. Fermin had meant to betray him, prevent Wolfe from using the formula on his own instead of taking on the Crown together, Wolfe was sure of that. Fermin had made his move just before Wolfe made his. But if his daughter thought this mishap was a mistake, and if she knew her father's code, well, who was he to disillusion her? "There's a small garage in the back, madam. If you bring your automotive there, I would be happy to help you unpack."

"Oh wonderful!" She twirled to the door, pausing in the opening to look back at him. "And please, call me Eliza."

II.

The pink liquid in the flask bubbled and churned over the burner as Wolfe delicately pieced more glass tubes to the distillery. Just a little bit more ....

The door opened, slamming into the wall with a sharp crack, and the tube shattered in his paw. He yelped in pain.

"Oh dear, I'm sorry, did I startle you?" Miss Eliza asked in a breathy voice, rushing over to grab his paw. "That's my fault, isn't it?"

Wolfe breathed in deeply, as much from her touching his wound as to take in her delightful scent. Though it had only been a short while since her arrival, he had decided that strawberries were most heavenly. "It's nothing, Miss Eliza. It will heal itself in a moment."

He gently removed his paw from her hand and placed the other on her upper back, guiding her to a plush high back chair. Books were piled around it: Fermin's notebooks, his own, and books for Miss Eliza's own amusement. The books on perfumes he could understand her reading, but why she found Whitaker's *Hormones, Pheromones, and the Senses* a fascinating read, Wolfe couldn't comprehend. Whitaker was barely literate! And his theories nonsense. As if any rational being would fall for such bestial trickery.

He turned his attention back to her. "You seem agitated though. What's wrong?"

"Oh, it's Inspector Grant again. He seems to think we're hiding evidence of my father's wrongdoing or some such. He's threatening to condemn the house!" Miss Eliza flung herself into the chair, taking a moment to arrange her skirts. Wolfe kept his mouth shut, lest his tongue loll out like a common dog and betray his amusement. "I've only been here a few weeks and he says the payments aren't up to date! You have been keeping the payments up, haven't you? I don't want to be out on the streets and have another of my father's partners locked away!"

Had he? He seemed to recall putting the payments in the post, but the days were a blur of experiments. He was the verge of the solution!

Miss Eliza hadn't noticed his distraction. "... and he wants to court me! How could I when—?"

"Court you? Who?" Who would dare to take his Eliza away from him?

Wait. *His* Eliza?

"Inspector Grant. Do try to keep up. But I shan't see him as long as the work remains unfinished." She laid a hand on his arm.

Wolfe growled. "Would you like me to take care of him?" He blinked and straightened. Take care of him? That wasn't what he should do. But now that he thought of it, it would be easy to do and an easy solution.

She gasped. "Oh no, you musn't, Doctor Wolfe! But … would you really be able to take care of him? Just for me?"

He stiffened. "As your father is currently … *incapacitated*, it falls to me to protect you in his absence."

"Even if I said I could protect myself?"

"I … I would insist, Miss Eliza." And he would. It was the proper thing to do, after all. One couldn't leave a lady to face an unwanted suitor on her own. It had nothing to do with her being far more competent than her father, with a much more delightful laugh, or that he found himself following that strawberry scent around the house when she went out. Or even that it was so rare to find a woman who could hold a proper scientific discussion. No, this was simply a matter of proper etiquette. Even if he was planning to skip right to a duel.

"I shall keep that in mind, good sir. However," she waved a hand towards his distillery, "I think you've left your chemicals over long. Weren't you trying Campion's distillation and tincture arrangement today? I do believe that has a shorter boiling time."

Wolfe rushed over to find the liquid had boiled over. He nearly threw his muzzle back to howl in fury, only to catch himself and slam his paws on the table, rattling the beakers and tubes. "Drat it all! It'll have to be redone!"

"May I help this time?" Miss Eliza approached, her skirts gently brushing the carpet with the sway of her stride, and stood at his elbow. "It's the least I could do after causing you injury. Besides, didn't I tell you Campion's methods were outdated? While traveling in France I heard of this amazing new method to combine chemicals, but we'll need to modify my aether engine."

The scent of strawberries intoxicated him. "For you and science, Miss Eliza, I am willing to try anything."

III.

The bright blue liquid in the flask sat calm and still. Wolfe eyed it warily. Had they done it? Was it right? He couldn't remember what color the original potion had been.

It was stable though.

He had followed all the instructions as Miss Eliza had read them.

It smelled delightfully of strawberries.

So it had to be correct, right?

His head ached. Thank goodness for Miss Eliza. The—what had she called them?—formulas he once knew looked like arcane scrawling now. Words slipped off the pages of his books and he had to be careful not to rip them apart in a fury. Why was his mind abandoning him now? Now at the edge of victory?

But it would be all right after this. Drink the

potion and everything would be fixed the way it should be.

They would go forth and take the Crown from the silly queen upon the throne, and he would prove to Fermin and all the scientific heads what *true* science meant.

Then he would ask Miss Eliza to marry him. She would be *his*.

The door opened and she stepped in. "Haven't you taken it yet?"

He shook his head. He was getting ahead of himself. "I'm not sure if it's right. It doesn't look familiar."

"It'll be alright, Wolfe!" She walked over, the swish of her skirts sounding enticing over the hum of the aether engine in the back of the room.

They had ended up using it to … to …. He groaned. Word. What was the word? They had twirled it. That worked. Twirled it in a circle to separate some of the components better. Her idea. She'd make an amazing assistant for any man. However she was in front of him, holding up the flask.

"We followed my father's instructions perfectly, and yours as well. This will make everything right. Your head will stop hurting." She laid a hand on his arm.

"I know, I know! I just …." He groaned again and gripped his head. Strawberries. Focus on her. On the success.

She huffed and then smiled as he looked up at her. "I just want to see my father's mistake corrected. Drink it. Please."

"Just one more test. After the last time," he

waved a paw at himself, "I want to make sure there's no more problems."

"But what test would you—?" She ground out before a loud banging resounded from the front door. "Now who could that be? Do whatever testing you think you need. I'll go check the door." She left, leaving the door open behind her.

Test. Test. What test could he do? What test could he remember? He could ... see how it reacted on a plant. He had plants. But plants weren't animals. Wasn't that why he took it himself? The tests were inconclusive on other animals and plants weren't a good option. Maybe the aetheric microscope Miss Eliza bought? It would show any impurities in the formula.

Shouting. His ears perked up. Miss Eliza was shouting at someone. Wolfe padded to the open lab door and listened.

She was yelling, "... Grant, he's not here! Coming in will help nothing!"

"You have been evading me all week, Miss Fermin! I won't have it! Not with proof he's as dangerous as your father! Either he comes away from this house, or you do!"

Inspector Grant? He was threatening Miss Eliza! Wolfe growled and grabbed the flask. This was his mess to fix. He just had to get Grant placated. Then all would be well.

The potion chilled his throat as it rushed down.

Pain. Twisting bones. Tearing muscle. Blood rushing in a hot frenzy. Heart beating, hitting the bones in his chest. Something was *wrong*. The beaker shattered on the wall across the room. What had *she* done? He roared, the glass around him rattling from the pressure.

Footsteps running. Gasps.

She was in doorway, hand covering mouth. *Her* other hand was gripped by the man in front of *her*. *She* was pulling, tugging, escaping. Strawberries filled his senses: *she* was unhappy.

Growling. Man pulled out silver barrelled thing. No matter. Leaping, tearing, biting.

Screaming.

Silence after crunch. Hot liquid rushing down throat.

She laughed and petted head. Red coated *her* skirt. "Oh my gorgeous *Wolfe*. You've given me the world!"

Sniffed. Strawberries. Tail wags.

The Yellow Butterfly

Ashley Capes

Clank.

Takashi slammed his hammer in time with the other men in the factory. Light from high windows gleamed on the steel sheet. Another ten just like it had to be finished by dark, else Shachō Nishimura would have two men—chosen at random—beaten and sent home without pay. His brutes wouldn't break arms or legs of course, since it wouldn't do to hurt productivity, but the bruises would be black enough.

And maybe it wouldn't matter soon.

The town of Baigan was teetering on collapse, or so it seemed. He'd tried to buy pears yesterday, and the merchants had only shaken their heads and sent Takashi back to the dust that climbed the wooden walls of the buildings around him. Shouts had risen from the harbour as he'd walked by but he hadn't turned. Another submersible accident – more of Nishimura's lust for gold gone to folly.

A shrill whistle sliced through the clash of steel-on-steel and hiss of steam.

Takashi stopped, wiping the sweat that stung his eyes. It ran down from his close-cropped hair; like every sane man in the factory, he kept it short. Less to get caught in one of the hulking, snapping machines – their mouths were ever-hungry. There was always someone shovelling piles of coal into the beasts' red bellies and their sparks were like tiny orange demons, darting everywhere.

It was different in Geinmo, supposedly, where electricity powered some of the machines. Takashi sighed; a new world loomed.

Foreman Ito entered through the gate. His face was red and his arms flapped in his black kimono as he strode along the rows of sweating men. "Shachō Nishimura is on his way. I want you working, do you understand? Don't make me regret hiring you." He shook his head, then hollered. "Two more submersible interiors due by the end of the month. That's ten days. Ten days!"

Hiro set his hammer down and leant close, grinning. "He seems especially shrill today."

"That he does, my friend," Takashi said. "Maybe he can no longer afford fruit either."

"No. I saw his wife returning from the market in Geinmo; they still manage to find good food."

An engine rumbled outside, followed by the now familiar hiss of a steam-wheel coming to a halt. Ito ran to the box-like office near the open entrance and jerked on the chain beside it. A dragon-shaped whistle screamed, and then it was back to work.

Clank. Clank. Pause, breathe. *Clank. Clank.* Pause, breathe.

Takashi swung his hammer in time with Hiro and the others, glancing at the entry as he did. Nishimura eventually entered the room, clothed head-to-toe in western garments: a suit with jacket, pants, shiny black boots and a ridiculous domed-hat concealing his silver hair. What did they call it? A bowler. Whatever that meant.

Fool.

But then nearly all the ex-Samurai were. They'd scrambled to find some way of maintaining power for years now. And for many, that meant business. Flying machines, submersibles, steam-wheels for land and rail, and even the new, motorised weapons. For others it was straight to the army. Where Father said he ought to have gone. *It is the duty of the strong to protect the weak.*

Nishimura spoke to Ito as he strolled down the line. The factory-owner's eyes swept across the floor but didn't truly appear to see any of it, as if his mind were elsewhere.

"... and you have not experienced any such problems?"

"No. No infestations of ants, Shachō," Ito said, a look of confusion passing over his face. "I keep the factory clean of insects and vermin, in fact—"

Nishimura raised a hand. Ito stopped speaking. "No matter, Ito, truly. It was an idle question; you know how I loathe such insidious creatures. And you need not concern yourself with the state of the factory."

"Shachō Nishimura?"

"I am closing it. Baigan is finished; work is moving to Geinmo. It's bigger and there is more opportunity for growth. The future of trade is no longer in submersibles in any event: it is in flying machines and steam-wheels. The latest model can carry four passengers; we only need the roads to improve."

"This is unexpected, I mean, we haven't even had time ...."

The two moved beyond ear-shot, voices buried by the clash of steel. Takashi stopped. Closing the factory? What would happen to everyone? Maybe Baigan was dying but that didn't mean the old snake had to drive the nail into the coffin.

"What's wrong?" Hiro asked. The other men were still pounding their part of the steel. "Why are you stopping?"

"You didn't hear?"

"No."

Takashi gripped the handle of his hammer. "He's going to close it."

Hiro took him by the shoulder. "Speak louder."

"He's going to close the factory," Takashi said, raising his voice.

The other men in his row stopped. "Who?"

"Nishimura."

Movement at the entry caught his eye. A young woman ran into the factory, her yellow kimono flashing in the patch of light. Takashi lowered his hammer. The way she moved ... such joy. Her silky black hair had been cut to frame her face and her eyes sparkled. Even the butterflies patterned on her clothing seemed alive.

It appeared she smiled simply because she could run.

Chou. She bore the same demeanour whenever he happened to catch a glimpse of her in the market square. Kiku had been the same; the innocence of childhood.

"Father!" she called after Nishimura.

Hiro nudged him, and Takashi returned to his work. They soon finished, and he moved to the pile of flat sheets, lifting it with another man, and returning to set it in place over the frame. This, like all the others, they'd curve to form the inner-lining of the huge passenger submersibles that took people all over the world.

The latest design boasted a clear bottom for observing the sea floor; the glass several *shaku* thick. Or 'feet' as those engineers who had returned from the west now said. Not something he'd ever book passage within – even had he the money.

By the time the small group returned, Ito was nodding again as Nishimura explained which pieces of machinery would be sent to Geinmo by rail and which would be sold.

Nishimura's daughter walked alongside, her head down, hair hiding her face.

The butterflies on her kimono no longer seemed to dance.

Hiro nudged him again and he returned to work. "I'm going to ask Ito about the factory closing. It can't be true," he said.

Takashi only nodded. He counted syllables as he hit the steel; he still had no ending that satisfied him but the poem was taking shape.

thistles dancing —
an autumn wind
muffles the long road

###

Ito had been powerless.

The factory closed as the leaves fell across the pale hills behind Baigan, and the men began to leave, searching for work. A few to Geinmo, some north to the mountains, others east, where word had filtered down: the Emperor needed steel workers for his new project, a great moving stair that would climb Fuji-san. Hiro was going to try his luck.

"Come with me," Hiro said where they stood before the iron-covered harbour. A sea breeze ruffled their clothing and tugged at columns of rising smoke. "There will be work – a dozen of us are travelling together."

Takashi shook his head as he watched the great crane on the dock, its squat body puffing steam as it struggled to lift the insect-like shape of one of the newer, sleek submersibles. The sides were fitted with long, thin cannons for torpedoes. Men waved flags and shouted as they coordinated. "Thank you, Hiro, but I will remain here."

Hiro sighed. "Are you sure?"

"I am. This is where she would have wanted me to stay."

"You can't live your life this way forever, in a dream, waiting for a tomorrow that won't come."

The man was right, but Takashi only shrugged. "All my memories of them are here. If I leave, there will be nothing left."

"Take your memories with you."

He put a hand on Hiro's shoulder. "A new place means new memories; the old ones will be replaced. Here, I hold them a little longer. Go, go to the Emperor and build his stair. It will be marvellous; you'll be happier there."

Hiro's expression fell. "Take care then."

Not until his friend's footfalls had died away did he turn back to the buildings. How small and fragile the wooden walls appeared compared to the stone and iron of the harbour. Or the watchtower beside the hulking walls of Nishimura Manor where it glared down upon them all.

He started toward the market. With what little money he had left he would buy his own tools and maybe the blacksmith would take him on.

Takashi passed through the shadows between the two-storey buildings, the eaves of peaked rooves extending over the street. Birds chattered from the thatching overhead but their songs were soon drowned in the bustle below. A patchwork of people filled the market: reds and blues, pinks and greens of kimonos and robes, but also the more muted greys and browns of western dress, their voices calling for goods before the storefronts.

The clock-master had closed his shop, but a pair of children had set up a blanket before it, selling pieces of broken machinery: springs, cogs, nuts and bolts all slick with grease. Caps and valves—he even saw a copper coil of wire. Where had they found that? One of the wrecks in the water? He did not ask, did not let himself think upon sunken submersibles.

He slipped through the crowds. His broad shoulders made it easy enough; people moved aside, sometimes after a glance at his expression. Sometimes without looking. Yet he didn't mean to frighten anyone.

He purchased a new tool belt and an old rivet-gun, the pressure-metre covered in dust.

Next came food. The catch was poor. Fish continued to die in the dirty harbour, and the prices were so high that he moved to the grocer and asked for the usual rice and fruit. He snared the last of the peaches, which was a stroke of luck, and smiled when Kenji wrapped everything and placed it on the bench before him, the older man brushing away a few grains of salt as he did so.

"Two *ryō*, Takashi."

Takashi hesitated. "Two?" He'd calculated less for everything he needed and could only pay for the rice. Or only the fruit.

"Prices had to go up again."

"Then I cannot pay for both, I'm sorry, Kenji. Keep the fruit; tomorrow I will—"

"Let me," a woman's voice interrupted.

Nishimura's daughter stood beside him. She held out a few smooth pieces of gold to Kenji, who accepted the *ryō* with a bow. "Lady Nishimura."

"You know I prefer 'Chou', Kenji."

An older woman stood behind Chou; she clicked her tongue. "And the young lady should not be troubling either of you."

"It's no trouble," Chou smiled. She set a jar upon the bench as she spoke. Ants covered the inside, moving in and out of the earthen shapes within. "Aren't they wonderful?" she asked when she noticed his gaze. "Look at how well they work together."

He nodded. Perhaps they were, in their own way.

"Do you keep them?"

"Yes, I'm building them a home, only I need a bigger jar already."

The older woman sighed. "And we should continue that task now, My Lady."

Chou waved a hand. "Soon, Kama. You're one of the men from the factory, aren't you?" she asked Takashi. "I'm glad I could help you, especially now that Father is closing it down."

Takashi nodded. "I am, but I cannot accept, Lady Nishimura." He bowed.

"Don't be foolish." She smiled up at him. "Let me. In fact, tell your friends if they will meet at the harbour, by the wreck, tomorrow at dawn, I will help them too."

Chou's servant frowned but only pulled Chou away from the stall. The young lady's yellow and purple kimono was swallowed by the crowd. Takashi looked to Kenji. "How could a man such as Nishimura have a daughter like that?"

Kenji raised a steel tin and spun its handle. Cogs ground within, and the lid flipped open. He slipped the coins inside. "He is not her father by blood, you know. Orphan. Took her in at the insistence of his late wife. Few talk of it anymore."

"I see." Perhaps that explained why the man didn't seem to care for her.

He drifted away from the market, visiting the Smith, who wasn't able to make any promises. "It all depends on who stays. Maybe you should look at Geinmo. Or further south?" And then Takashi found as many of the old workers as he could, urging them to meet Chou at the harbour come dawn. Few seemed to believe much would come of her offer.

Some seemed as desolate as he—especially the older men—while others were packing their possessions.

And still he could not join them.

Instead, he headed for the glistening water. Better than sitting at home—the empty walls, the empty table, the flowerbed shrinking to grey.

His footsteps counted the syllables:

thistles dancing –
an autumn wind
drowns out my heart

Before dawn he met several more men where they stood together in the grey light by one of the old submersibles. Rust ran from its huge rivets. Patina discoloured the body and grime ringed the portholes, obscuring the controls within: a forest of levers and gear shifts, none of which he'd ever truly understood.

Maybe it would be better never to see another made here.

Deadly machines. Not just for the navigators and passengers, but whole towns, like Baigan, where they had left only misery in the frothing wake of their waves. He greeted a few of the men and listened to their talk. There was little confidence in Chou but the same thing brought them here – desperation, perhaps, more than curiosity.

And she did come.

Before the sun broke free of the horizon Chou appeared, her servant in tow. The older woman carried a chest, her weary face tight with strain. She dropped it to the deck with a sigh. Muffled clinking followed, and the men exchanged glances.

Chou smiled at them. "Thank you for trusting Takashi; I am glad you have come to meet me. I know my father has made your lives difficult in closing the factory. In a small way, I hope to help." She paused to nod to her servant. "Kama has small piles of *ryō* wrapped in cloth. Each of you take one and let it help you on your way; for if you take gold you must leave Baigan. My father will not be pleased."

One of the men spoke. "And we can simply take them and owe you nothing?"

"Yes."

Takashi frowned. "Lady, if you have taken this from your father ...."

"Do not worry. By the time he discovers it missing it will be too late."

A voice spoke from the end of the pier. "Or very nearly too late."

Nishimura raised a lantern, turning a tiny lever to increase the brightness. It lit the dull faces of half a dozen men, all armed with long *tachi* and smaller knives. Two also carried modified matchlock rifles. A thin shaft jutted from above each weapon, a dial on the side. With it, each man could load and fire half a dozen rounds far quicker than usual. Another terror of the new world.

The gathered factory workers fell silent, and Chou let out a gasp.

Nishimura gestured for two of his men to take the chest; a third he directed to Chou, after a glance to Kama. The servant's wrinkled face did not change, but Chou spun on the older woman. "Why?"

Kama glanced away.

The third man took Chou by the arm, wrenching

her around and dragging the young woman toward her father. She cried out, and Takashi took a step forward.

One of the riflemen raised his weapon.

Taskashi stopped.

"And now, gentlemen, I trust you will continue to seek employment elsewhere." Nishimura turned his glare upon his daughter, then cut the lantern light. He turned to leave, and their shadows receded along the boards, the figure of Chou struggling against them.

Takashi ground his teeth but did not follow.

They'd only shoot him—or worse, hurt Chou.

Two days passed, and he ate the rest of his food and spent the last of his money. And not once did she appear in the market, nor did anyone in Baigan hear from her. Not Kenji or any of the other shopkeepers. Not even Ito, who Takashi stopped as the man attempted to close his door on the second evening. "Takashi, listen to me: I don't know anything. I'm sure she's well." The man's jowls seemed to sink further toward his chin, and he could not meet Takashi's gaze.

"Ito, don't lie. You dined there last night at Nishimura's invitation; you must know something."

"I know he's offering to move me and my family to Geinmo."

Of course. "But you didn't see her?"

"No, Takashi. Now go home. And change your clothes for God's sake. You smell terrible." He slammed his door.

Takashi shook his head. Not at the comment

about his clothing—it was true, he needed to change—but at the lie. Ito knew something. And of course the man was afraid to speak: his future depended upon staying on Nishimura's good side.

Takashi wove through the front garden with its red maples and turned down the lane beside the house, angling toward the square. He'd reached the edge when a creak echoed in the lane. A gate swung open, and a woman stepped out. Ito's wife.

She waved him closer, hands slipping from the sleeves of her blue kimono. She had tied her obi in some haste, as her sash sat a little crooked.

"Haru-san?"

"Quickly," she said. Her voice was hard to hear over the murmuring from the market and the roar of a steam-wheel passing somewhere nearby. "My husband was upset when he came home last night—I fear Nishimura has hurt Chou."

A chill spread across Takashi's body. "He what?"

"Yes. But do not ask any more, Takashi. A darkness hangs over him since his wife died."

He folded his arms. "Then you should not have told me."

"No, that is *why* I tell you. Your name was mentioned: Shachō doesn't like that you are asking after Chou. Make your peace with it, return to your life."

Takashi smiled. "I have had no peace for years." He thanked her and headed for the square.

"You cannot bring them back, Takashi, not this way, not any way," she called.

He offered no answer.

Instead, he returned home, lit his lamps and removed his clothes. He wiped himself down with a wet rag, stepped into a fresh kosode, then brushed at the sleeves of his haori before pulling the coat on too. Then he ran a razor across his jaw. A tiny spot of red bloomed in the mirror, and he wiped his cheek with the back of his hand.

Finally, he knelt by a screen then slid it aside.

And blinked.

Ants.

Ants had crawled within, finding a crack, a space between timber and earth: like smoke or water, somehow they'd found a way. And there they covered the floorboards before a steel chest.

Swarming in place.

They moved in a pattern, like a kanji painted by a rough hand. It seemed to spell out the word for 'tower.' He leant closer; there was no doubt. That was the word. And there was only one tower in Baigan, the tower beside the manor. The building looked across the ocean and collected signals from the flashing mirrors when the submersibles rose.

And so there he would go.

He lifted the lid of the chest and drew out a blue silken scarf. A boat with a single sail crossed the waves. This he took and tied around his forearm. "Shima ..." He could not finish. Would she approve? Yes. She had to. Next, he lifted a child's *hagoita*-paddle covered in cherry blossoms. Kiku would have urged him on. "You would have liked Chou," he told his daughter.

He hooked the paddle in his belt.

Finally, he lifted the new smith's hammer from where it leant against the doorframe and walked into the darkening night.

He did not lock or even close his door.

He did not pace out syllables nor answer those who spoke to him. He skirted the market and climbed the small hill to the manor where it overlooked Baigan. The grand home sprawled: its tall stone walls were split by a huge gate of banded wood, but the yellow glow from dozens of paper lamps within still crept over the barrier.

The tower loomed nearby.

A black shadow against the stars, chill silence spread from its stones. He climbed the rough-cut steps to its twin doors. A rusty chain and lock were looped through the iron handles. Why lock the doors? Surely the tower was still to be manned; after all, boats and ships still sailed to the harbour.

He raised his hammer and smashed the lock.

From the manor came nothing but the drifting notes of court music played on flutes and the *biwa*.

Takashi ground the doors open and stepped within, boots crunching on gravel. The dark lay about his shoulders as a heavy mantle. He gripped his great hammer and hefted it. Here was the tower. Where the ants had directed him.

What lay within?

He turned to the wall and searched a moment—a lantern. He lifted it free and struck the lever, the little device shooting sparks. But light followed, a steady glow that lit a cluttered room. Tables and crates lay stacked beneath a winding staircase, but at the very back, behind a pair of torn screens painted with snow, something glinted in the light.

Steel? He moved closer.

Brass.

Takashi crossed the floor and shoved one of the screens aside. It clattered to the stone.

A large brass chest rested beneath a frayed blanket. It had slipped free so that the brass caught the lantern light. He pulled the covering aside. Another lock on the lid, but this, too, he smashed with his hammer.

And then he could not move.

Could not lift it.

Nor even reach forth to lay a hand on the cold, gleaming surface.

He exhaled; he'd been holding his breath, and his throat had tightened. There'd been no such moment for Shima or Kiku. Only the sweeping blue roaring of the ocean, waves tipped in white. Only a terrible absence coming home. He had to open the lid.

A yellow butterfly rested within.

Chou lay upon her side in the brass coffin; a great, dark bruise covered her temple. Her eyes were closed and her skin pale. No smile graced her lips. The stillness was complete; even his shadow seemed to shrink away.

"No."

She had deserved better.

Takashi spun with a cry as he hurled the lamp. It hit the wall with an orange burst. He strode back into the night, hammer held in white knuckles as he bore down on the bright manor.

And he counted syllables as he stalked.

my spirit set adrift —
butterflies dance on
the autumn wind

Aubrey in the World Above

Daniel Lind

Our stagecoach rattled across the rough ground. Then it stopped. Father looked at me through his monocle; his solemn stare had an unearthly quality, making my stomach quiver. The final day had arrived.

Father sat opposite me, holding his top hat and cane. He removed his monocle, and his haunting eyes branded my insides like they always did. "Your mother is a thief. Don't follow in her footsteps." Father tapped his cane on my shoulder. I flinched.

"We will also discuss new household arrangements," he continued. "You shall wear maid's clothing. It does not befit a young lady to wear a jacket and trousers." He pointed at my legs with his cane.

I couldn't say much. Father always had the last word in every argument, and I didn't want to start one now. But I couldn't resist.

"She didn't steal that hen!"

Father shook his head and climbed out the carriage. He motioned with his cane for me to follow. The drab, thick, fog smothered the street and Town Square. A large crowd of men, women, and children had gathered.

As Father and I reached the centre, I noticed the heap of sand lying there. Hooded monks and, behind them, a row of nuns approached the mound. The procession floated out from the cathedral gates on hover decks. I wanted to rush over there, kick the sand away, and scream at the monks.

I watched in horror as electricity sparkled in a static rhythm underneath the decks, following them in a glimmering tangerine trail. The monks surrounded the heap, chanting in an ancient language. Around one of the monks' neck dangled a locket. He opened it, exposed a polished green bean, and planted it into the mound. A tremor sizzled through the square like butter on a hot pan.

"Leave her alone," I yelled between sobs. I thought I had prepared myself for this day, but I couldn't hold back the tears. Mother had been clad in a rugged sack. Her hands and feet were tied like a captured deer ready for slaughter. Two monks dragged her through the drizzle of rain and placed her onto the mound.

"What will happen to her?" I asked.

Father scowled. "She'll serve the Giants."

"How will she manage?"

"The matter is out of my hands."

The crowd cheered and applauded the morbid display. Following tradition, a tall man in a black suit sold steaming mince pies to the wealthier clientele.

From a barrel strapped on his back he served lemon tea. The smell of meat and lemon made my stomach churn.

"Why can't you do something?" I asked Father.

"Enough questions!" Father raised his cane and an umbrella extended with a swoosh, shielding him from the rain. "It is about to begin."

Tiny cracks appeared around us, blemishes on a rough surface. The fissures popped like balloons through the cobblestone, and raced towards the centre where Mother sat. The audience's cheer grew louder.

Rows of cavities surrounded the centre mound. The ground vibrated. Then a crater opened next to Mother and through the dirt exploded a magnificent stalk.

The plant grew to an enormous size in one breath, reaching for the sky. It looked like it would touch the moon. Gentlemen in the audience stared in awe—one of them dropped his tea cup. People jostled in front of me. I couldn't see what the monks were doing, but I had brought a pair of zoomers and took them out from my satchel. Mother trembled in front of the stalk. Her eyes were closed, and her long dark hair covered her face like a dirty blanket. "Mother!" I yelled at the top of my lungs.

The stalk's jagged leaves, branches, and roots, ensnared her. They pulled her inside the mint green plant like a thousand searching tongues. Amber sap dripped onto the ground.

When the stalk had completely swallowed her, silence reigned for a moment. Gentlemen in expensive leather coats were still busy chewing their mince pies, dropping crumbs on their ties. Then the monks and nuns lowered their heads and hummed in unison, as if helping the plant to digest Mother. Through my shaking zoomers I saw her silhouette fading inside the trunk. I screamed for her again, but it was too late—she had been devoured.

The following weeks, I slaved as a scullery maid: cooking steaks, serving tea and scones to Father's business associates, cleaning rooms, and wiping floors. My room had turned into an antiquities storage, and I'd been permanently moved to the cellar kitchen, a hellhole of leaking pipes and stringy cobwebs nestling in the ceiling.

My own place was under the kitchen sink. I huddled inside at night, piecing together scrap metal into a mechanical hen I called Pecky, remembering Mother's desperate look before she disappeared. I used Pecky to mend anything broken around the house; more often than not the sink leaked, and I'd wake up drenched in water and the latest nightmare.

Father put a plate with leftover scones outside the sink every evening after his guests had left. My appetite had completely disappeared, and I only frowned when I spotted the scattered crumbs. They always smelled of stale tobacco smoke, and the plate had red wine stains.

Prominent British businessmen were invited tonight. With a deep sigh, I gathered plates and spoons on a silver tray and removed a lemon cake from the delivery box; the guests wanted their dessert. With slow steps and shaking hands I entered the dining room, balancing the full tray. Four gentlemen sat and talked around the table. Thick smoke puffed from their pipes. Silver plates with half-eaten steaks, pateés, and scone crumbs littered the tablecloth.

Closest to the door sat Father. He gave me a grim look. "Why's it taking so long? Our guests want lemon cake."

I recognised the man sitting next to Father as one of the monks attending Mother's Ascension. A locket with the symbol of the Stalk dangled around his neck. My heart nearly stopped. The monk sized me up like a broken spare part and said, "My condolences. Your mother had no choice but to serve in the World Above. A child bereft of a parent, however, is always tragic."

There had to be a bean inside that locket. If I could somehow—

"Aubrey!" roared Father. "Bring dessert and tea."

This was my chance. I bowed and raced down to the kitchen cellar where Mother stored her recipes and herbs. There had to be something that encouraged ... sleep.

I needed chamomile and lavender. I also needed cactus juice, oils, and a spoonful of sugar to sweeten the concoction. With searching hands I turned the jars inside the wooden cupboards until I found what I needed.

"We are waiting!" rumbled Father's voice upstairs. "Don't make me come down."

The lavender needed to be ground. Where the mortar?

"Aubrey! Now!"

I moved dirty dishes from one corner to the other, took stock of drawers and cupboards, but to no avail. Father would come any minute and punish me for not having the tea ready.

The screeching of a moving chair came from above. Heavy footsteps. I reached for Pecky and wound her up, letting the hen pluck the lavender as much as possible while I rushed and locked the cellar door.

A moment later, a bang came through. "Why have you locked the door? The guests are waiting, Aubrey, and I am becoming impatient."

"I'm preparing the tea, Father, but I spilled it and need to change clothes."

I returned to see how Pecky was doing; the lavender stalks had been crushed, but it wasn't enough. I mashed the remaining ingredients with my palms and mixed them into a bottle with chamomile, lucuan oil, cactus juice, and a squeeze of lemon. The pungent odour twisted out of the bottle.

I prepared the cups on another tray, together with a porcelain pot for the tea. Father banged on the door again, startling me, and I dropped a spoon on the floor.

Holding the tray in unsteady hands, I unlocked the door. Father adjusted his monocle when he saw me, his frown relaxing. "We will discuss your attitude in the morning," he mumbled. "Bring the tray upstairs."

"Yes, Father."

Inside the dining room again, I poured tea to each gentleman, making sure the monk received a few extra drops. They needed to sleep long enough for me to reach the Town Centre.

Father appeared in the doorway, a long black pipe sticking out of the corner of his mouth. A dark shadow played on his face, moving between his chin and eyes. "My Aubrey needs to learn manners," he sneered. "She behaves too much like her mother."

I lowered my head. "Your tea is ready, Father." The sooner he'd drink with the others, the sooner I could escape.

Within minutes, Father and his guests slouched on the leather sofa, pipes dangling from their slack jaws. I snatched the monk's locket, grabbed my satchel from the cellar, and dashed out onto the street. Horse carriages clattered past me, and strolling gentlemen eyed me with scowl in their eyes: my escape had already caught too much attention. I hurried into somber side streets, and dreary alleys where stinking fish racks lined the crummy walls. A factory whistle blew somewhere.

Town Square loomed in the distance. Someone shouted my name. I spun round and spotted three monks on decks, hovering towards me. One held a sack in their hands. With a wild flutter in my chest and no time to think, I sprinted towards the Square, nearly tripping over on the cobbles.

The sound of my heartbeat thrashed in my ears as I opened the locket and removed the bean. My fingers trembled as I placed it inside the new mound and stepped back. The angry voices and the decks' humming came closer. Within seconds, the mound sprouted emerald and jade. Leaves and sharp thorns sprawled from the ground. A plant emerged from the cracks and grew in size until it reached the clouds.

"Aubrey, I forbid you to Ascend!" echoed Father's voice.

Thorny branches grabbed and twisted my waist from behind. With one swift motion, the plant drew me inside its belly.

I stumbled out of the pod and fell onto soft ground. Sap drooped from my ripped garments in long strands across the cloudy surface. The chilly air stung my bare arms.

A floating plume, shimmering in lilac, approached me in a pirouette and wrote *Your name?* in the air.

"Aubrey," I answered with a cough, spitting out leaves.

The quill searched for my name on a parchment hanging in the air. I didn't understand what it wanted and must've looked confused; the quill pointed its sharp end at me and scrawled *NO SUCH NAME.*

"You're a funny one," I said. "I'm not here to serve. I'm off to the Giant's castle." I tapped my satchel twice, and Pecky poked its head out and chirped.

Follow the footsteps wrote Quill and hurtled towards an emerging stalk in the distance. A trail of indented footsteps appeared, leading into the horizon.

The Giant's castle was an enormous construction, nothing like I'd ever seen in the World Below. Its front towers were curved patchworks of rustic copper and steel, with spiny wires and massive cogwheels keeping everything together. I examined the castle wall: a hodgepodge of metal bolted together, as if a child had thrown together a toy house in a hurry. Steam billowed from rusty pipes, sticking out from the walls like pins in a cushion. It had several gaps, large enough to squeeze through. A row of pennants waved at the top of each tower.

"Mother's there. Why don't we take a look?" I removed Pecky from my satchel, wound her up, and released her. The hen's olive eyes lit up, and she wobbled through a gap in the wall.

The castle courtyard looked more like a scrapyard. Bundles of metal in all shapes and sizes littered the ground. Bolts and screws, big as boulders, lay on top of the metal heaps. The castle entrance was blocked by an assortment of planks, but one of the towers looked good enough for climbing.

The ascent to the top was more difficult than I'd expected. The metal plates were sharp, cutting into my legs and hands and scraping my cheeks whenever I rested my head on them. I bit back a scream and lost my grip, nearly tumbling down. At the last moment I clung to a pole and pulled myself up. Fear splintered my heart, but I couldn't give up now.

I dragged myself through the open window and collapsed on a wooden floor. A musty smell of old garments hung in the air. A bed that would room twelve grown men stood empty in the corner, along with an unpolished mirror hanging on the wall. The ageing dresser had a thin layer of grease and dust covering its knobs and handles. No sounds came from outside.

"Are we in the right castle?" I asked Pecky inside the satchel.

I searched for a crack in an oversized door and found one I could squeeze through. My expectation to find servants and cleaners bustling around the castle like busy ants was wrong. Pecky chirped and bounced inside the satchel, so I took her out and placed her on the floor. The corridor was ornamented by exotic animal heads hanging on the wall.

The hen wobbled forwards, and I edged behind it. We arrived at the end of the hallway to a set of two enormous doors, one of them ajar.

"Is there someone inside, Pecky?" I whispered.

The spacious throne room had a lush carpet stretching in all directions, and a table made out of polished wood stood in the centre. A Giant hunched on a marble chair with a dozen buttons and metal levers attached to his seat.

The Giant rose from his seat and said, "You're clever, little one. Once, a naughty boy entered me land to steal me grandfather's harp and hen. Are you here to steal too?"

"I'm not a thief," I replied. "Neither is my mother."

"The gentlemen Below delivered a notice to Freithos. They explained your theft to reach me kingdom." Freithos pushed a brass lever next to his throne, releasing multiple rattling cogwheels. A wide net covered me from above.

The web pulled up with me swinging inside it. I was trapped like a wounded animal. "Release Mother," I shouted with a gasp. "Father is a cruel man with hatred nesting in his heart. I'd rather serve here with Mother than slave in the World Below."

Freithos grinned, exposing colossal teeth like stalactites in a cave. "Humans can tell any lies. Me wife trusted the boy who came here long time ago, but me does not."

"Please, Freithos, listen to me! I've come with a gift – a new hen."

"A hen?" Freithos' bushy eyebrows raised to this forehead.

"Pecky," I said. "She'll serve you well." I opened my satchel and set Pecky loose. It pecked, nibbled, and jabbed the net until it gave in and both of us fell out, landing on the carpet with a thump.

"That's a chicken!" roared the Giant. "I have no use of that."

"She's a mechanical hen that will help you around the castle," I said. "By the looks of it, you might need it." I turned the knob on Pecky's back, and with a whirl it pecked the carpet clean of dust.

The Giant inspected the carpet for a moment and said, "Me shall release you in exchange for the hen and send you to the World Beyond."

Freithos pulled a bronze lever. A ticking clockwork with emblazoned symbols and dials appeared through amber steam on the carpet. In the centre sat an emerald stalk. "Your mother awaits you inside," said Freithos and motioned for me to step inside the clockwork.

As soon as I entered, the world changed into scarlet and azure, glinting into a haze of warm colours. I lost track of time and space as my bearings disappeared into a rainbow. When I finally came to my senses, I sat at the dining table in our house. Mother sat beside me, a silver napkin spread across her knees. "You are right on time for supper," she said with a smile.

"Supper?"

Through the door came a procession of servants, led by Father in a grey beanbag. They carried trays with steaks, vegetables, and exotic fruit.

"May I serve chicken soup?" asked Father with

low voice. His monocle had disappeared and around his neck dangled the symbol of a Giant.

Story Origins

How many did you guess?

The Clockwork People-
Pinnochio

The original story about a wooden puppet that came to life was created by Italian writer Carlo Collodi. Angela Castillo decided to rewrite the story with clockwork dolls, therefore creating a steampunk twist.

Perfection-
Bluebeard

To him, Steampunk—indeed, any of the "punk" genres—has always felt like something darker than similar styles, and so when the idea of a steampunk fairy tale was brought up, what came to Chris Champe's mind was more in the realms of The Brothers Grimm than Walt Disney. "Bluebeard" felt like a story that could be adapted to fit a steampunk setting very well, and through the course of writing it, it started asking a question about humanity: at what point was Doctor Blaubart no longer terminating a failed experiment, but instead murdering his wife?

The Mech Oni and
the Three-Inch Tinkerer-
The One-Inch Boy

Dave here! *The Mech Oni and the Three-Inch Tinkerer* is a retelling of the popular Japanese story, *Issun Boshi*, or *One-Inch Boy*.

Issun Boshi has many versions, which take place in different regions of Japan. We chose Hokkaido as the setting, since we called that island home for a year. We not aware of any other retellings that take place in Hokkaido.

Although set in Japan, we kept the language and cultural references minimalistic. *Ganbatte* is what Japanese people say to wish each other luck. While thinking back to my semester in Sapporo, I remember a young Japanese woman who was helping us withdraw money motioned for us to come to the desk. To everyone's confusion and amusement, the Americans and I sat down, since the Japanese hand gesture for "come here" is the American gesture for "sit down." This is why Yuki points to her nose, instead of placing her hand on her chest, when she introduces herself.

One less subtle reference is Mr. Suenaga asking Issun if he was a *Koro-pok-guru*. *Koro-pok-guru* are tiny people in Ainu mythology that traded meat and other goods with the Ainu people. They didn't like to be seen, so when a young Ainu man, who wanted to know what they looked like, waited to ambush them, the *koro-pok-guru* were so offended that they quit trading and have never been seen since. One familiar reference in the Western world is the Picori from *The Legend of Zelda: The Minish Cap*, who live beneath house plants and leave gifts for the player. Since the Ainu are native to Hokkaido, and *Issun Boshi* is a tiny man, we felt the reference was appropriate.

We aimed to stay true to the roots of *Issun Boshi*, even though our *oni*, which is a kind of Japanese ogre, was actually a giant automoton.

The Copper Eyes-
The Crystal Ball

The Copper Eyes was inspired by a short story called *The Crystal Ball* by The Brothers Grimm. I came across it while looking for a piece to adapt for our collection. It was a happy mess, with every fairy tale element shoved into a two-page story. When I decided to work with it, I tried to make it more cohesive. The witch mother became the inventor mother. The 'Crystal Ball' became Oliver's goggles, which were used throughout this version. The animals became metal machines. The biggest change was Aileen. I wanted a female character that kicked butt instead of a damsel in distress stuck in a tower like in the original. So Aileen was created, and I am extremely happy with how it turned out.

Strawberry Sins-
Beauty and the Beast

This story started with "how would the Beast from *Beauty and the Beast* be transformed in a steampunk setting?" Perhaps because of my love of *Girl Genius*, the answer was "it was a science experiment gone wrong". Mad science and villainy soon followed.

The Yellow Butterfly-
The Dream of Akinosuke

The Dream of Akinosuke struck me as a story brimming with wonder and that touch of sadness that many folk and fairy tales hold. I tried to hold onto and expand that while bringing in the steampunk element. To do so, I needed to add a villain and technology, but I wanted to keep certain visual elements like the ants and the yellow butterfly from the original too. Hopefully together, it all adds up to something new!

Aubrey and the World Above-
Jack and the Beanstalk

This story is inspired by *Jack and the Beanstalk* with a dark twist. It contains references to the original where Jack was a villain. There are also influences from other fairytales such as *Cinderella.*

As a child I was influenced by the Swedish author Astrid Lindgren's tales (my favourite being *Mio, my son*), and I've tried to instill some of that atmosphere here.

Author

Information

Angela Castillo

There's magic all around us, if we just know where to look. Angela Castillo has a goal as an author: to help people see. She comes from the small town of Bastrop, Texas, where she loves to walk in the woods and shop in the local stores. Castillo studied Practical Theology and Music at Christ for the Nations in Dallas, Texas. She was home-schooled all through high school and is the oldest of 7 kids. Castillo's greatest joys are her little girl and two boys, who 'are the best inspiration for writing ideas.'

Angela has several books available in paperback and on Kindle, including short stories, middle-grade fiction, and historic fiction.

Excerpt from *Hidden Pictures, Twisty Little Short Stories and Poems: TAMER*

Evening approached and with it, blessed relief from heat and the road. The circus troop made camp within a few miles of a small town, the morning's destination. People sank into makeshift beds of canvas and straw; animals fidgeted in heavy chains and cages riddled with filth.

Geneva made tiny squeals behind her great trunk while she begged for a pail of water to splash over her tired body. She squeezed her massive hulk into the corner of the wagon. Clean by nature, there was no escape from the piles of her own waste.

The lion, Fanghorn, paced the twenty square feet of wagon he had called home since a cub. Growls rumbled from his emaciated body and sometimes evolved into roars which shook the barred walls. Every mile traveled by the caravan increased his misery.

Despite deep exhaustion from a hard week of work, precious slumber would not come to Lurkey, the circus clown. Errant bits of straw pricked into him and even turpentine failed to ward of the gnats. His muscles ached and nerves twitched along his back and shoulders. He gave up the fight and rose.

Lurkey glanced back at the other clown, curled up child-like on a bundle of canvas. Gustav's head was thrown back, mouth wide open in a snore. The man could sleep through anything.

He staggered out to the community water barrel in the center of camp. Lurkey withdrew the dipper and poured some into the tin cup hanging from a rusty chain on the side. He swilled the lukewarm water in his parched mouth, spit it out on the ground, and took another swig.

"Trouble sleeping?"

He choked on the water and dropped the cup. Coughing, he held his arms up over his head until air flowed freely again. The man in the shadows made no move to help him.

"Gosh, Ringwald," Lurkey gasped. "You almost skeered me to death!"

The ring master stepped into the dim halo of Lurkey's lantern. His top hat added ten inches to his already massive form.

"Stupid clown," Ringwald's grimace revealed a mouth full of rotten teeth. "Since you are rested enough to fetch water, you should get to work. Go muck out the elephant wagon."

Links:

http://www.amazon.com/Angela-Castillo/e/B00CJUELT0/ref=dp_byline_cont_ebooks_1
http://angelacastillowrites.weebly.com

Chris Champe

Chris Champe has been found primarily in West Virginia for the past few decades, rarely straying far from home unless brought further afield by the promises of anime or gaming conventions, large LARP events, or the occasional major hiking trip. He's mostly a fanfiction author and has only recently begun focusing on more original work.

He'd like to thank his wife Heather White for her support, editing, motivation, and inspiration, as well as constantly pushing him to overcome his laziness and actually finish a project.

Leslie & David T. Allen

Leslie and Dave are Pittsburgh, PA authors and caretakers to three unpredictable, and often demanding, mutts.

Inspired by the worlds and stories of David Eddings, Baldur's Gate, and Final Fantasy VI, they strive to imbue their fantastical stories with a dose of humor and plenty of intrigue.

On the rare instance they aren't writing, they forge ahead on any of their other numerous obsessions, such as gardening, programming, and putting together Legos while watching Buffy the Vampire Slayer.

They are currently working on a character-driven epic arcane steampunk series called *Bitlather Chronicles*.

Links:

Find out more at http://bitlather.com

To receive notifications of new releases, sign up for their publications newsletter at http://bitlather.com/newsletter/fairy

Excerpt of *Dream Eater's Carnival*

It was an explosion—not the ringing of the bell tower—that startled Leisl awake.

By the height of the shadows, she'd slept through the morning bell. Not the first time she had neglected chores in favor of sleep.

She hugged a sheet to her body and hurried across the cold stone floor to peer out the arched window. A plume of smoke rose above the nearby field. She traced it to its source, a full-sized replica of a galleon ship. Iron-wheeled houses with colorful banners trailed the vessel as it crept toward town. The procession resembled a small village on the move.

Forgetting that only a thin sheet robed her nakedness, Leisl hurried to the cathedral observatory. There she grabbed an arm-length rosewood telescope and dashed to the balcony. Her elbows pinned the sheet around her while she focused the lens.

A sign crowning the tallest wheeled building read *The Tower*. Acrobats launched themselves through windows and twirled on poles jutting from the structure. One performer worked her way to the roof, where she did a handstand atop a flagpole. Another rode a unicycle balanced on a railing while he juggled.

This wasn't an invasion, it was a carnival. Precious few visited town anymore, and this one looked especially wonderful. Leisl smiled at the promise of adventure and returned her attention to the ship. Shreds of a sail whipped about the mast as it rocked back and forth across the bumpy field. She read under her breath, "The Dreamer's Carnival."

The sailors reloaded the cannons and fired another volley into the sky. Leisl flinched, hoping they were blanks. Performers on balconies tossed confetti and sweets to the cheering crowds that rushed to meet the procession. A jester saddled the carved mermaid bust and tossed life preservers to the townspeople.

"You are not decent," a pious voice announced from the gardens beneath her.

"Brother Mikkel, I was startled by the explosion …"

"Yes, and everyone else will be startled by your exposure. You are seven-and-ten now, and you still can't dress yourself?"

Leisl blushed and pulled her sheet tighter.

Music blared from the carnival. She watched the cheering crowd with envy. Their parents hadn't given them to the cathedral. Unlike her, they were allowed to have fun.

With one last glance at the performers, she returned to her dormitory cell. She didn't bother to get dressed, not yet. Brother Mikkel wouldn't check on her; he'd be too busy researching to notice if she attended to her work.

She continued to watch out the window, already planning her escape.

To read more, visit http://bitlather.com/books

Allison Latzko

Allison Latzko is a recent graduate with a degree in Fiction Writing. She lives in Pittsburgh, Pennsylvania, where she spends her time slowly writing horror novels she plans to someday publish. It's just taking quite longer than expected. The Copper Eyes is her first published short story.

Links:

Blog: https://allisonlatzko.wordpress.com
Excerpt from Allison's upcoming book: *Queen of Hearts*

Excerpt from *Queen of Hearts*

When I was younger and my dad was alive, he liked to frighten me with tales about the haunted theater we once visited called The Refuge.

"While many horrors have befallen the performers and guests of this theater within the last century," my father read aloud to me and my sister, "The Refuge still stands as one of the oldest, most popular, and most uncanny tourist attractions in Alden Grove."

He read from an article he'd found on a magazine page, exaggerating every syllable to make them all sound ominous and frightening. My sister Em and I were both awed by his voice, mesmerized like two young girls should have been. He had fun scaring us, telling us ghost stories before bedtime instead of fairy tales, and letting us watch Tales from the Crypt instead of Barney. We'd eagerly sit in the living room with him late on Saturday nights, watching movies like A Nightmare on Elm Street until our mother came home from work and made him shut it off.

To see something right from the Travel Channel's most famous haunted places was something I'd longed for. "Established in 1893" was marked on a gray and faded slab, which was tacked on to the corner of the brick building. I snapped a picture of the entrance to the theater and a short staircase that led to two gold and red doors awaiting our entry. I hummed ecstatically. It was a place I had only ever seen in my dreams.

"Will we see dead people?" I asked loudly, moving my camera away from my face. My family stood around me in a circle.

"No, Delaney. He's just scaring you. The magic show won't be like that," my mother said.

"Are you sure?" My thoughts swirled. "I think we're going to see some."

"Let's go inside." She took my hand and led me up the steps, her warm fingers pressed around my small fist. My sister and dad followed.

My dad spoke with false menace as we walked up the steps. "Most people say if you're quiet long enough, you can hear the dead screaming from hell as soon as you walk through the entryway." Our eyes widened in fright and he grinned back at both of us.

"Greg, you're going to give them nightmares before we even go inside." My mother stared around us with a look of contempt. My dad chuckled, checked his pager, and led us through the entryway. As we passed I read the 'no photography' sign posted at the entrance of the theater and tucked my camera into the folds of my blue jacket.

I had imagined a grand opera house-type theater that held hundreds, with seats scaling up the sides and balconies holding the most sophisticated theatergoers as they observed with small binoculars. Instead, we got a room with tables in the back and fold up chairs in the aisles. There were scuff marks in the floor and cracks in the walls. As I sat down, my dad's shoulder brushed up against mine. We were in the fourth row, close enough that we could see every detail on the stage, every indent in the floor, and every wisp of shadow underneath the stage curtain. Red velvet lined the sides of the walls and the lights danced above. It was just nearing sunset outside, but it was eternally nighttime inside the theater.

I drummed my fingers against the side of my ripped chair cushion. As we waited for the show to begin, a man appeared on stage. My sister and I leaned forward in our seats, whispering excitedly. "Is that him?"—"Is it starting?" My dad put a finger to his mouth to shush us, although I could tell there was a hint of excitement on his face. Only our mother looked uninterested, gazing at the man as though he were an annoying bug crawling on the counter.

The man wore an ill-fitting suit, and his large face was very pale and sickly. "Thank you everyone for coming tonight for a very special show at The Refuge" he said, coughing into his sleeve. "I have some unfortunate last minute news: our regular magician will not be performing tonight. He's gotten terribly sick, and has had to cancel at the last moment."

The crowd murmured and lost focus of the stage. Dread welled up inside of me. I glanced around and felt the disappointment of the audience, some of whom had known about the magician's act. Others looked towards him with confusion. Friends from my class had been chatting about the magic show all week, and after my onslaught of begging, my parents had granted my wish. Now everything was falling apart. I slid to the edge of my seat and waited, hoping with all my might that the show would go on with any magician necessary.

The large man continued. "Instead, we'll be introducing two new last-minute performers who we assure you are worth everything you paid for. Please welcome your magician, Quincy Ganson, and his lovely assistant, Elizabeth Armonte." The crowd clapped but I couldn't help notice a ripple of disappointment throughout the room. People stood and walked back toward the door as dismay stirred in my chest.

A young man and woman appeared on the stage and it took a moment for the audience to notice. I elbowed my sister Em, who'd been looking at the family beside us that'd gotten up to leave. The man on stage, Quincy, was tall, and his shadow stretched out behind him. His suit looked expensive, and he wore a red tie that matched the dress of his petite assistant. His eyes roved over the crowd. The woman looked to be about a foot shorter than him, but side-by-side the two couldn't have belonged anywhere else. They matched like two pieces in a puzzle.

"Ladies and gentlemen," the magician called out.

"Are you ready to see something amazing?" No one cheered. Everyone was fixated on the family walking out. "Suit yourselves," he added.

The doors swung back and forth, and another couple stood to leave.

"You two are going to miss out," his assistant Elizabeth called in a high-pitched voice, which echoed through the building. She placed her hands on her hips as she watched them with an amused smirk. The light from above gave her dress a blood red sheen and her short black hair curled against her round, childlike face.

Lifting her small hand above her head, she snapped her fingers.

It was like a firework had gone off, bursting in the auditorium. A few people yelped. I blinked and Elizabeth was no longer where she'd been on the stage. I glanced around nervously, then towards Em, who shrugged back.

The back of the theater gasped.

Elizabeth stood in front of the doorway and ushered the couple back to their seats. Em and I glanced at each other, our smiles widening and faces lighting up. The magician began to clap and, slowly, the audience followed suit. When Elizabeth was back on stage beside him, he grabbed his hat, swung it and bowed.

"Now are you ready to see some magic tricks?" Quincy asked, and everyone cheered. The show had officially begun.

Heather White

Heather White hails from the lands of the Appalachian Mountains. She spent her childhood moving, giving her a love for books, games, and stories and driven her passion for twisting tropes. Her writing passions run towards the paranormal and the romantic with an emphasis on superheroes. You can find out more about her and her other projects at her blog: https://heatherwhiteauthor.wordpress.com/.

She'd like to thank her family—Mom, Dad, Jay, Andrew, and Daniel—for their support and belief all these years.

Ashley Capes

Ashley is a poet, novelist and teacher living in Australia.

He's the author of six poetry collections and five novels and was poetry editor for Page Seventeen from issues 8-10. He also moderates online renku group Issa's Snail.

Ashley teaches English, Media and Music Production, has played in a metal band, worked in an art gallery and slaved away at music retail. Aside from reading and writing, Ashley loves volleyball and Studio Ghibli – and *Magnum PI*, easily one of the greatest television shows   ever   made.

Links:

http://www.cityofmasks.com
https://twitter.com/ash_capes
http://www.amazon.com/Ashley-Capes/e/B004H6WC4K
https://www.goodreads.com/author/show/5806251.Ashley_Capes

Excerpt from: *A Whisper of Leaves*

Riko unclenched her fist when the plastic of her phone cover creaked.

"Damn it."

She dropped it on the empty passenger seat and took a breath. Relax, idiot. Smart phones aren't cheap. She gripped the steering wheel of her little Toyota instead; was he ever coming out?

Parked beneath the shade of a pine tree in one of Fuji-Yoshida's better neighbourhoods, it probably looked like she was on a stake out – the family who'd circled the block in the afternoon sun had certainly given her an odd look.

But she didn't have a choice; her job was at stake, maybe more.

And the man who held everything in his palm was doing his best to stay out of sight. Ikeda's compound – the residence was more than merely 'fenced' – had cameras, intercoms and a massive gate that remained closed to visitors. He had to leave sometime. Or return, if he was out. And she'd waited hours – she wasn't going anywhere, especially after nearly getting lost finding the place.

What would she even say? He'd be angry. And he wouldn't believe her; why would he? Her word against that of his son. She was a fool for trying.

Riko jumped when her phone rang. She grabbed it.

Dad.

"No way." Not now. She jammed the mute button down and tossed the phone back onto the seat. Even if she could talk, he wasn't going to say anything she hadn't heard a thousand times before. Worse than a broken record – he was like some awful, auditory tattoo.

A black Lexus, sleek as a gymnast, pulled into the driveway. Riko jumped out of the Toyota and dashed across the road, slipping between Lexus and gate. The driver, a man in a dark hat and suit, hit the horn and inched the car forward.

Riko stood her ground. "I need to speak to Ikeda-sama."

The driver pulled on the handbrake before winding the window down. "What are you doing?" he called.

"I need to speak to Ikeda-sama. It's important."

He stepped out of the car, leaving it running. "He doesn't take visitors. Best if you get out of the way, young lady."

"Please."

He shook his head, then looked over his shoulder. "Shachō?"

A back door opened and a short man exited. Of an age with her father, his hair matched the jet black frames of his glasses. A blue tie sat bright against the grey of his suit. "Konda? What is this?"

"This lady here wants to talk to you. She won't move, I'm sorry."

Riko gave a bow. "Ikeda-sama. I wanted to speak to you about your son."

The man's expression morphed from annoyance to suspicion. His narrowed eyes tracked her as she stepped closer. Konda too, kept a close watch.

"How does this regard Yuuki?" Ikeda's posture would have brought a coat rack to tears.

"I taught at —"

"Enough." He held up a hand. "You are Riko-san?"

"Yes. And I came to swear to you that I never acted in an inappropriate manner with Yuuki."

Konda whistled, but looked down when Ikeda glared at him. To Riko, Ikeda said, "This is a poor apology."

"It must be hard to believe, but I'm telling the truth. Maybe the pressure on him was –"

He shook his head. "You do not hail from Japan originally, do you? I hear a slight accent. English? No, Australian perhaps?"

She frowned. "My parents are from Hokaido, but they moved to Melbourne before I was born."

He nodded, showing no pleasure at his guesswork, skilful as it was. "Then you are here on a work permit."

"Yes, but that doesn't have anything to do with what happened."

He smiled. "Do you think so? My son is not a liar. Should you wish to remain here in Fuji-Yoshida, in Japan for that matter, you will keep away from my family and my home."

Remain in Japan? Could he actually get her deported? "But –"

"Understand, Riko-san, that I will not have this disgrace fall upon the Ikeda name. Consider yourself fortunate that you were only dismissed."

"That's not –"

Ikeda pointed at her. "Not another word." He climbed back into the Lexus and snapped an order. The gates rattled open and Konda returned to the driver's seat, giving her a look. A warning? Part sympathy – it was so fleeting she couldn't be sure.

Riko stepped aside and the car lurched forward.

And that was that.

Read More here:

http://www.amazon.com/Whisper-Leaves-Paranormal-Novella-ebook/dp/B00X8TKZ4Q

Daniel Lind

Daniel is a teacher living in the United Kingdom with wife and two children. He was born and raised in Sweden but emigrated in 2007. He's previously had short stories published in magazines such as Pidgeonholes and Zetetic and a zombie western is forthcoming in Flash Fiction Press.

Links:

Twitter: https://twitter.com/lindhoffen
Facebook: https://www.facebook.com/lindhoffen

Excerpt from upcoming sci-fi story
The Givers – a novella:

The steel door shut behind me as I entered the cramped room. Two teenage girls sulked at a desk. One had piercings all over her face, and her long hair shimmered green and blue. The other wore make-up that would turn any member of Kiss green of envy. Both wore torn black jeans and smelled old clothes.

I sat on a chair in front of the girls and nodded. "Does it hurt?"

The pierced girl glanced at me with utter disgust. "Wha'?"

"The stuff in your face," I said. "Does it hurt?"

She scowled. "The fuck d'you care?"

I shook my head. "Sorry. I'm Nathan. Apparently, you two were in my store last night. I'd like to know why."

The girl in make-up lifted her head from the

desk. "We didn't—"

Her friend shushed her. "Is that what your alien buddies told you?"

"My apologies, I didn't catch your name." I extended my arm.

"Alice," said the girl with piercings. "And she's Charlotte."

"Can't your friend speak for herself?"

"No."

"All right." I scratched my head. "You claim you didn't trash my store. Why were you there then?"

"You're no blueberry, and no lawyer." If her voice carried poison, I'd be dead now. "So why don't you piss off?"

Feisty teenager—exactly what I didn't need. I cleared my throat. "We're gonna be here a while, d'you girls want anything to drink?"

Alice reclined in the chair and showed her middle finger with a grin. Charlotte had her head on the desk and didn't move.

"My surveillance outside the store recorded you two breaking in. That's a criminal offence."

Alice sighed. "Like I told the other geezer, we were asked to go and get something. The back door was open!"

I lost my train of thought for a moment. "You were asked? By who?"

"One of your alien buddies. Jack, Joshua, or somethin'."

Joseph.

I leaned forwards. "What did he want you to take?"

"Cameras."

Why would the Givers take my cheap cameras? If

they needed them they could've done it themselves—
no need using teenagers as bait.

Printed in Great Britain
by Amazon